House of Vamp
Uprooted

Book 2

By

Jesse McDowell

Copyright © 2016 by Jesse McDowell

All rights reserved.

Edited by Victoria Perkins

Cover design by Jesse McDowell

Headshot by Robert Mannis / RobertMannisPhotography.com

No part of this book may be reproduced in any form or by any electronic or mechanical means including information storage and retrieval systems, without permission in writing from the author. The only exception is by a reviewer, who may quote short excerpts in a review.

This book is a work of fiction. Names, characters, places, and incidents either are products of the author's imagination or are used fictitiously. Any resemblance to actual persons, living or dead, events, or locales is entirely coincidental.

Jesse McDowell

Visit my website at www.jessemcdowell.com

Published by Jesse McDowell Chattanooga, TN

ISBN-10: 0989317536

ISBN-13: 978-0-9893175-3-5

"I choose not to see the world in an Age of Coming or an Age of Going, but rather in an Age of Present."

- Rupa Vamp

CHAPTER ONE

Di Vamp stood in front of the Beverly Hills mansion where she had lived, on and off, for over a century. Of all of the places she'd resided over the course of her seven hundred plus years, this one hadn't been any more or less special than the rest, but the people she loved called it home. They were what made home for her, not a building, and their well-being was the most important thing to her.

A gentle breeze tugged at a few wayward strands of dark hair and Di shifted the large umbrella she was using to keep the California sun from hitting her skin directly. She could feel the heat beating down on her and knew that, even in a full pantsuit, she would need to find better shade soon or she'd end up with a sunburn.

Di sighed as she motioned to a spot of red paint that one of the groundskeepers, Thomas, had missed. She didn't have to say anything for one of the others to get it. Her staff were watching, always watching, especially the ones who were new. She understood the anxiety, of course, as well as the anger and fear that had prompted the mess she was currently supervising clean-up for. She had, after all, been around during the Salem Witch Trials and many other instances of people's fear of the unknown.

The night before had been just one such example. Vandals had lobbed cans full of bright red paint over the gates. Fortunately, nothing was broken, but paint covered the grass, trees and flowers. It had dried in rivulets down the Greek columns and seeped into the minute cracks of the stone-paved walkways. The house that had stood as one of the city's most unique historical architectures since before its founding in the early nineteen hundreds now looked like something out of a horror movie.

That was the point, Di supposed. For centuries, vampires had been the boogeymen, the monsters in the dark. Then, they'd become the moody, angst-ridden romantic heroes that, for some reason, made certain people even more angry. Now, they could be either one. But that was in fiction. The Vamp family wasn't fiction. No, they ran one of the most prestigious fashion companies in the country. They hired the best designers to bring their ideas to life, the top models to showcase them, and headlined at the biggest fashion shows. It had been after New York's fashion week that they'd been given the chance to show the world the truth. Well, as much truth as could be found in a reality show. And not that most people believed what they saw was the truth. Despite some very obvious situations, there were those who refused to admit that *House of Vamp* was anything but a publicity stunt by a rich, eccentric family.

Di glanced over at the cameraman who'd been filming the clean-up. Apparently, this wasn't exciting enough to get much airtime in the second season. It made sense as the news channels had been all over this and the other 'incidents' that had occurred in the two months since the late Hiram Whet had announced the renewal of the show. She supposed they were hoping that the Vamps would react with violence, but that wasn't their way. Or, at least, it wasn't what the head of the family would allow, and no one defied Heir Vamp.

While Di watched, the new cameraman – Harold if she remembered correctly – smoked his cigarette and eyed the backside of one of the new maids. Di wrinkled her nose in distaste. While vampire senses weren't quite as powerful as some fiction made them, they were enhanced enough that Di found the scent of tobacco repulsive. In a far back place in her mind, she thought she might have once liked something that smelled similar, back when she had been human, but Heir's mother had turned her so long ago that Di's memories of her fifty-five years before becoming a vampire were a bit hazy. Though, she suspected their upcoming journey might prompt those memories.

Her eyes narrowed as Harold flicked the butt to the ground. Almost as if he could feel her glaring at him, he turned. The color drained from his face and he quickly bent to pick up the butt. The camera that had been leaning on his hip started to fall and he only just grabbed it before it would've landed on the rocks lining one of the walkways. Red flooded back into his cheeks, turning them a strange mottled color. Di had a moment to think of how lucky Harold was that the whole uncontrollable blood lust part of vampire lore was only partially true. She could practically see his pulse pounding in his throat.

Harold was visibly flustered as he looked around for a place to put his cigarette. Finally, he dropped it into his water bottle, but after a few seconds, realized he didn't have anywhere to throw that either. Face flaming even brighter, he grabbed his camera and hurried away.

Di turned back to the house, showing none of the discomfort she was starting to feel. While vampires didn't burst into flame when touched by the sun – or do other absurd fictional things – direct light would result in painful burns that could, if bad enough, cause entire layers of skin to peel away. She still had a ways to go before she got that bad, but it wasn't going to be pleasant from here on out.

"Ms. Di?" An older man approached her.

"Yes, Flint?" The head groundskeeper had been with the family for years, and while he'd never come out and said it, Di was fairly certain he knew that the Vamps were exactly what they claimed to be.

"I know you have a lot of packing to oversee too, so if you'd like, I can supervise the clean-up from here."

Di regarded him shrewdly for a moment. She did all of the hiring and never brought on anyone she didn't feel she could trust.

Flint had proven that loyalty just a couple of months ago when an unfortunate incident in the backyard had resulted in a police investigation, but she was still going to take a moment to make sure he didn't have an angle. Di wasn't cynical or hard, but she also wasn't stupid. Finally, she nodded. She did have a lot of work to do.

Flint headed off to continue the task and Di headed back in to the house. Heir was in London with his middle son, Alexander, which left Di in charge of getting the rest of the Vamp family ready for their trip. While she usually was the one who organized and planned, Heir being around gave an extra sense of authority. The Vamp children all respected and loved Di, but their father was the undisputed head of the household.

Di had known Heir his entire life. Literally. Unlike her, he'd been born a vampire. His mother, Rupa, had turned Di at a time when fifty-five was a decade beyond the average life expectancy. Heir had been born just a few months later and Di had taken care of him from the beginning. As with all natural born vampires, Heir had aged slowly, growing into a child, then a young man – teenagers were a foreign concept back then. He and Di's friendship had evolved as well, turning from her as an authority figure to a confidant and friend. There had never been anything romantic between the two of them, not even when Heir had moved into middle age and then passed her. He'd finally Settled at the age of sixty-five, and was now married to his third wife and father to six children. With his silver hair and wise eyes, he was the perfect picture of a patriarch.

As she entered the mansion, Di found Heir's third wife standing by what appeared to be three steamer trunks, six full-sized suitcases and nearly a dozen smaller bags and cases. Valencia Vamp was the only other Turned vampire in the family. She'd been friends with Heir's oldest daughter when they'd been the same age, but she'd remained human until years later when Heir finally turned her and made her a permanent part of the family by marrying her. She had no children with him, but loved each of the kids and did her best to be a mother figure to the younger four.

Val's main weakness was her fear of looking old. She'd been able to pass for forty back when she'd first been turned, but modern technology had promised to make her look even younger and she'd embraced it whole-heartedly. Di could smell the blond hair dye that Val had to use every couple weeks to maintain her color. Apparently, it was touch-up day.

"Do you really think you'll need all of those?" Di gestured towards the bags. "You do know we can purchase things if we needed them?"

"We're going to be gone until January," Val said. The skin on her face was stretched so taut that it looked like it would crack if she tried to move too many muscles. "I just want to be prepared."

Di shook her head, but didn't argue. She knew Shianne, and possibly Erickson, would have just as many bags. Maybe it was a good thing that the network had insisted on chartering two Boeing 747's, one for the family and one for the crew. Di hadn't been happy about that at first since the Vamp's sleek, black jet had custom-tinted windows that allowed the Vamps to move about freely without fear of the sun, but the network had assured them that all of the necessary precautions had been taken. She'd hired two men to make sure of that, and they'd reported back that all was well. It still didn't make her like the idea any more. She didn't trust that the network hadn't hidden cameras on the plane to catch what their cameramen couldn't. She'd already seen how they'd manipulated things through editing, and the first season hadn't even finished airing yet.

Val's dark eyes flicked behind Di, the motion conveying that cameraman Harold was doing his job again. Since the entire premiere ball debacle, all of the Vamps were a bit more cautious around the cameras. It wasn't anything a human would notice, but even the youngest Vamp would've caught on.

A crash and a shout came from upstairs.

Speaking of that youngest Vamp...

Di hurried towards the stairs, cameraman following.

CHAPTER TWO

The room looked like a tornado had hit it and Prussia Vamp was feeling rather pleased with herself. She'd managed to get all of the clothes she'd need for their trip into two duffle bags. It wasn't until her phone started ringing that she realized the problem with the disaster area that was her room. She swore and began digging through piles of junk. By the time she found her phone, the call had already gone to voicemail.

As she straightened, she caught a glimpse of herself in the mirror and scowled. Her face wasn't flushed because that didn't really happen to vampires, but her bright red hair was half-way out of its normal sloppy ponytail, standing up at haphazard angles. Her bright yellow t-shirt must've caught on something when she'd been searching for her phone, because there was a jagged hole in the side. She was going to have to change.

She grabbed the closest shirt from a pile of discarded clothes and swapped it with the ruined one. This one was brown and had a picture of a snarling monkey on it. She smiled. She liked this shirt. She'd gotten it last month when she and her friends had gone shopping for new clothes. Her smile faded and the light in her emerald green eyes went with it. She hadn't needed the clothes because she'd outgrown her old ones, but rather because her stepmother had insisted Pru's wardrobe needed updating. Pru still had the thin, pre-pubescent figure of a twelve year-old that she'd had for years. Like all Natural vampires, she aged very slowly. The youngest of the Vamp family, even she hadn't been born in this century or the last. In fact, she'd been born near the beginning of the one before that, in the late eighteen twenties to be exact. In nearly two centuries, she'd only reached the physical and emotional age of twelve.

For years, she'd feared Settling at this age, being forever stuck between childhood and being a teenager. Never old enough to be taken seriously, but old enough to want to be. Pru yanked out her hair band and let her hair fall past her shoulders in all its wild glory. It had been bad enough befriending humans and seeing them age, but last month, something had happened that had made everything worse.

Leo had aged.

Born in the early eighteen twenties, Leo was the closest to Pru in age of all the Vamp siblings. He'd been fifteen for a couple of decades, his black hair and blue eyes never changing. Then, suddenly, last month, his face had lost some of its baby roundness, making him look even more like their handsome eldest brother

Erickson. He'd grown two inches, making him taller than Alexander. That was how they moved up a year in age. Their bodies would be changing so slowly that it would appear that nothing was happening for years, maybe even decades, then everything would happen in a short period of time.

Of the six Vamp siblings only three had Settled. Firstborn Erickson had settled at twenty-four in the nineteen twenties. Shianne settled in the nineteen forties at twenty-six, and Alexander, who was the fourth born, had settled in the nineteen fifties when he was nineteen. That left twenty-one year-old Taylor Ann, Leo and Pru still aging. There was a chance that all three could end up older than one or all of their Settled siblings, or they could Settle at the ages they were now. It was impossible to know until it happened.

Pru's phone buzzed with a text from the same person who'd called her. Karson Dee. If someone had told Pru six months ago that a text from tween heartthrob Karson Dee would make her smile, she would've bit them. Then, she'd actually bitten Karson and been forced to fake a romantic relationship with him to avoid the press freaking out. It actually hadn't been as bad as she'd feared. Despite his fame, he was a sweet guy and he'd obviously had a crush on her. She didn't feel the same way, but he'd known that. When their PR people had given them the go-ahead to end the relationship, Karson had been kind and understanding. It had been that more than anything that had made Pru want to keep his friendship. She suspected he still had a crush on her, but he kept it platonic, so she didn't mind. In fact, it had been Karson, more than anyone, who'd kept her sane when Heir had announced that Leo was now sixteen.

"Pru, you should not be playing on your phone when we need to be preparing for our trip."

Pru didn't even have to look back to know it was Leo standing at her door. She turned anyway. She loved her brother, but he'd always been a loner so she'd never felt like she knew him as well as she knew her other siblings, despite being the closest in age. These last two months, however, he'd been more active in what was going on, more present in conversations rather than lost inside his own head. And he was happier than Pru had ever seen him. If she hadn't been so frustrated that he'd aged, she might've enjoyed the change more.

"I'm done packing," she said, pointing to her bags.

Leo looked doubtful. "That is all you will need?"

"Yes, Leo," she retorted. "That is all I will need."

She plopped down on her bed, the movement causing a pile of clothes to bump against the table next to her bed. Before she could make a move, her lamp fell to the floor with a crash. She cursed more loudly than she'd intended as she went to see how bad the damage was.

"Is there a problem?"

Di was next to Leo less than a minute after the lamp had fallen. No surprise there, Pru thought. Di had a knack for knowing when any of the kids were about to fight. It came from having helped raise them, Pru supposed. Val might have been her stepmother, but Di had also been like a second mother to all of the kids, particularly the younger ones. The mysterious death of Treasa, Heir's second wife and mother to the four younger kids, had been harder on Heir than when Erickson and Shianne's mother, Kostya had died.

"No," Pru snapped. "It just fell."

Di looked at Leo who shrugged.

"I was simply inquiring if Pru had finished packing."

"I did." She pointed at her bags again and waited for Di to tell her that it wasn't enough.

Di sighed. "Please tell me you packed at least one nice outfit to change into for when we see your grandmother."

Pru nodded. She might like to push her boundaries here with her family or even with the TV show, but she wasn't about to do that with Rupa. It had been a very long time since she'd seen her grandmother and she wasn't entirely sure what to expect. She hadn't told anyone she was nervous. Her brothers and sisters would think she was being silly, and it wouldn't have done any good to talk to her human friends. Having a thousand-year-old gypsy for a grandmother wasn't exactly the kind of thing a human could relate to. And now that she thought about it, she wasn't even entirely sure how old Rupa really was. Heir had been born in the mid thirteen hundreds and Rupa had been in her late teens or early twenties at that point. Depending on how fast she'd aged, Pru reasoned that her grandmother could've been born any time between eight or nine hundred to as late as the first millennium. However the math added, Rupa had been around for a very, very long time.

Di gave Pru a critical look. "Brush your hair before we leave." She turned to Leo. "Where are your things?"

"In the car."

Of course they were, Pru thought. This was Leo's dream come true. The Vamps were heading back to Europe. The second season of their show would be focusing on the one thing Leo had spent his entire life trying to research: the history of their family.

CHAPTER THREE

Leo had never really understood his family. They spent so much of their time in the human world that he often wondered if they had forgotten what it was to be vampire. Val and Di, he understood to an extent. They had once been human, but Leo and his siblings had never been anything other than what they were now. He did not understand how they could be so fascinated by the trivial matters of the human world and have no interest in the truth of their own origins. For decades, he had been searching for answers to where they'd come from, answers to his mother's so-called suicide. Now, thanks to a bizarre twist of fate, it would be humans who would send him to the places he needed to go to get those answers.

His usual sense of decorum had been steadily fading as the day of their departure had drawn near, and now he found himself more elated than he had ever been. Finally, after all these years, he would be on the path to the truth.

"How much time until we depart for the airport?" Leo asked Di.

He had, at his father's request, attempted to alter his speech to something more modern, and had done quite well, but when he was not consciously choosing his words, he had a tendency to slip back into the speech patterns of his childhood.

"I have to go see how everyone else is coming along," Di said.

"I will check with Taylor Ann, if you would like."

Pru and Di both stared at him. He understood their surprise, but did not acknowledge it. He had no shame over his past behavior and none of his family had ever held his reclusion against him. It was just who he was, who he had always been.

"That would be very helpful, Leo, thank you."

He nodded, flashing a rare smile at the pair. Pru rolled her eyes, but he saw a hint of her smile, the one that twisted his slow-beating heart for it was then that she looked most like their mother. He hurried down the hall before he could dwell on his loss. He knew he was not the only one who had grieved over Treasa Vamp, but he could not think of it as anything but *his* loss. Over two hundred years and the pain was as fresh as the day he had seen her body being taken away.

He knocked on the door to his middle sister's room and, for once, tried not to think about the past.

****

Taylor Ann walked past the space where her full-length mirror had once hung. It had come down the day after her epic breakdown. It was easier to think about that now. Her family had rallied around her, supporting her, and one of the ways Heir and Di had done that had been to follow the network's suggestion and hire Stephen Young, an addiction counselor who also specialized in eating disorders.

Stephen had saved her life, and for that, Taylor Ann was thankful. The fact that she was grateful said how much he had already helped her. He spent two hours a day with her and was on-call the rest of the time. As he'd just left his previous practice when Di had found him, she'd been able to persuade him to take on Taylor Ann full-time. It had turned out to be money well-spent. In just two months, he'd gotten her on a regular, albeit still-restricted feeding schedule. He'd explained that it was better to ease her back into eating normally rather than expecting her to consume a normal amount of blood immediately. While the rest of the family ate every three to four days, she only ate once a week, but it was real blood and not those pills she'd been trying to use. This week, Stephen wanted her to eat with the family at regular intervals, though he was allowing a smaller portion.

Taylor Ann knew that her family had already started to see a difference. She could feel her body changing. Her bones no longer protruded so badly through the skin that they looked like they'd break through at any moment. She could see that on her wrists and knees, feel it on her ribcage and face. It had been a struggle to feel her clothes getting more restrictive, though Stephen insisted that they were now fitting as they'd been meant to, or at least, how they'd been meant to fit someone who was supposed to be the size she was now. She wasn't sure how she was going to react when she had to go up a size. She was keeping it together now, but she still didn't have the strength to look at herself in a mirror.

She ran her hands through her hair as she looked down at the two suitcases she'd finished packing and smiled, pleased with herself. Two months ago, she wouldn't have had the strength to close them on her own. Now, she could even carry them downstairs by herself. Her fingers caught in a tangle, and even that made her happy. She picked apart the tangle and reached for a hairbrush. The damage she'd done to her hair had been the easiest to rectify. Massive conditioning and the nutrients from real blood had turned her previously stringy and brittle reddish brown hair soft and shining.

"Taylor Ann?" Leo's voice immediately followed his knock.

"Come in," she said as she pulled her hair back into a ponytail. She turned as the door opened.

"Di wanted to inquire if you were prepared to leave?"

"I'm packed," she said. "But Stephen's not here yet."

She saw the brief shadow cross Leo's eyes and knew that it wasn't anything personal. In fact, it said something about how much her little brother cared about her that he didn't say anything about the fact that her human counselor was coming with the family. She supposed if she'd been feeding off of Stephen, Leo would have objected less, but she didn't feed from Stephen. She made a point of only feeding from anonymous donors Di sent to her. While the family fed off of their willing staff members, Taylor

Ann didn't feel comfortable enough to do that, not since she'd lost control and drained one of House of Vamp's most promising designers.

She frowned. She didn't like to think about what she'd done to Sky. She knew her actions had been a result of her addiction and starvation, but it didn't make them any less her fault. She thought that was one of the reasons she'd trusted Stephen almost instantly. He'd made her understand that she wasn't a bad person, but he'd also never babied her. She appreciated that. She didn't need someone to coddle her like some fragile, broken thing.

"Taylor Ann?"

The concern in Leo's voice brought her back out of her head. The fact that he, of all people, had noticed she'd gone off on a bunny trail meant she'd been really out of it. "Sorry, Leo," she said. "Just thinking. What were you saying?"

"I was simply inquiring if you had given Dr. Young a specific time to be here."

"He prefers to be called by his first name," she said. "And yes, I told him to be here at three."

Leo reached into his pocket and retrieved a watch. It was an antique now, though it still looked as good as it had when Heir had given it to his youngest son on Leo's twelfth birthday. It had been brand-new then.

"It is ten minutes to the hour," he said. "I do hope the good doctor is punctual."

Taylor Ann's mouth quirked up into a bemused smile. "I'm sure he'll be on time, Leo."

Her brother nodded, his eyes taking on that faraway look that meant he'd disappeared into his head. It always made Taylor Ann sad to see that expression. Her baby brother had always been a quiet child, one who preferred to play by himself rather than making friends, but the death of their mother had done something to him that no one had been able to fix. These past two months, in anticipation of the trip, Leo had been more present than she'd seen him since before their mother had died, but there were still times, like now, when he'd retreat into himself and leave without a word.

Taylor Ann sighed as Leo walked away. She could sense the tension around her father and Di whenever Leo brought up certain things he was hoping to uncover on this trip. She had no doubt that the two meant well, but Taylor Ann hoped, for Leo's sake, that he found what he was looking for. She really wanted to see her little brother happy.

CHAPTER FOUR

"You have to admit, Erickson, the network's timing is perfect." Shianne Vamp spoke to her older-younger brother even though she was studying herself in the mirror rather than looking at him. With her thick blond hair, baby blue eyes and pretty face, most people wondered why she wasn't one of the family's models like Taylor Ann. The answer was simple. No one told Shianne what to wear. She was the trendsetter, the fashion icon.

Case in point, she thought as she picked up another can of fake tan spray. Her idea to market her own line of tanning products had been a gold mine. Despite the flack she'd gotten about the name, Vamp Tramp Spray was a huge success. She was already looking into creating her own Vamp Tramp scent, and then was seriously considering a foray into shoes.

"What do you mean perfect?" Erickson was lounging in one of the plush, rose-pink chairs Shianne had added to her room last month.

Shianne turned away from the mirror to face her brother. "I mean, the paparazzi are worse than ever. We can't even go to a club anymore without getting mobbed by fans and reporters, and we're only eight episodes into the first season. We need a break."

Erickson tapped his finger against his titanium-plated fangs. He'd gotten them done just before the New York Fashion Show and Shianne was wondering if he was regretting it yet. Like her tanning spray, Erickson's accessory had sparked a frenzy among the vampire-obsessed humans. When she and Val had been going in for their surgeries, they'd seen at least a dozen people asking about having fangs surgically implanted in their jaws.

Shianne looked down and frowned. She'd been hoping her bandages would be able to be off by the time they left. She'd bought dozens of tops specifically designed to show off her beautifully vamp-tramp-tanned enhanced cleavage, but it looked like they'd have to wait at least another few days. She gently cupped her breasts and looked back at Erickson.

"They don't really feel much bigger. Maybe I should've gone with two cups sizes rather than just one. What do you think?"

Erickson raised one perfectly sculpted eyebrow. "Are you seriously asking your brother to check out your boobs?"

"Didn't you ask me two nights ago if your pants were tight enough to show off, and I quote 'what I have to offer'?" she retorted.

Erickson grinned, his hazel eyes sparkling. "That is true." He gave Shianne a critical once-over. "Two sizes would've been too much. You would've been like one of those top-heavy dolls that always look like they're going to fall over."

Shianne smoothed down her dress and looked in the mirror again. She had to make sure the bandages didn't make her look lumpy. "Thanks."

"I have to ask though," Erickson continued, his voice taking on a serious note. "Is Val bringing Dr. Frankenstein with us because she wants him to do another bust lift, or whatever it was he did?"

Shianne crossed to her bed and sat on the edge, putting her feet on one of her suitcases. "You know he hates that nickname, right?"

"I know," Erickson replied, his grin saying that he didn't care.

"And, no, Val isn't planning on having Dr. Darcy do another surgery. She's just worried that if she needs some...help while we're gone, she won't be able to find someone as capable."

Erickson frowned. "Doesn't it bother you that he used to be her lover before she turned him? I mean, that's weird, right? Our stepmother bringing the man she had an affair with in the fifties on a family trip?"

"If our father doesn't mind, I don't think we really have the right to complain," Shianne said. "Besides, we all know that Val and Dad don't...you know." She made a face at the thought of her father having sex.

"Stop right there." Erickson held up a hand. "That's not an image I want in my head."

"I don't know, Erickson, maybe thinking about Dad having sex could've kept you from the trouble you're in right now," Shianne teased. She picked up a magazine from her bed and tossed it at him. "The CDW's got to be eating this up."

Erickson glared at the cover. Her hair was dark brown now – probably her natural color – and she'd put on a little bit of weight, but pop superstar Tedi was still gorgeous. The pale pink baby doll dress she was wearing should have made Erickson leer, but Shianne knew that her brother wouldn't touch the singer with a ten-foot pole. Not again anyway.

"It's so unfair." Erickson sounded like a petulant child instead of someone who'd lived for three centuries. "What did I do to deserve this?"

Shianne sighed. She loved her brother. The two of them were closer to each other than any of their other siblings. After all, it had been just the two of them with their father and Di after their mother had died. Nearly eighty years passed before Heir remarried and then Taylor Ann had been born. They had both loved Treasa, and they loved all of their half-siblings, but there was a bond between the two eldest Vamps that none of the others could rival.

"You couldn't keep it in your pants, Erickson, that's what you did." Shianne crossed one almost-orange tanned leg over the other. At least her surgery wasn't preventing her from showing off her long legs.

"I thought you were on my side here, Shianne." He folded his arms across his chest.

"I am," Shianne said. "Wasn't I the one who went with you to those baby stores even after Di said we shouldn't play to the media?"

"Yes," Erickson said grudgingly. "But now..." His voice trailed off.

Shianne didn't say anything, her expression unusually serious. Yeah, now was the problem. The music video Erickson had starred in with Tedi hadn't done very well and he hadn't been asked back for a follow-up, but rumors had spread like wildfire that the playboy Vamp had been having a torrid affair with the pop singer. The pregnancy rumors had started shortly after that, prompted by Tedi's change in appearance and what appeared to be a sudden love of puffy baby doll dresses. None of the Vamps had taken the rumors seriously. They knew that the chances of a vampire-human pregnancy was extremely rare in a mixed relationship. The odds of it happening as a result of a slightly alcohol-induced, one-time seduction were miniscule. It happening with a Settled male vampire was impossible...or at least that's what they'd always thought.

Then Ibrahim Demir had called yesterday. Fortunately, Erickson had been the one to take the call, or Di would still have been yelling at the Vamp. Lawyers claiming to represent Tedi had contacted the Vamp family lawyer saying that Tedi was indeed pregnant and that Erickson Vamp was the father. And if that wasn't bad enough, she was claiming that he'd taken advantage of her. They also said they had pictures of Tedi with bite marks on the side of her neck. Erickson had told Ibrahim the truth – or at least most of it. He'd brought champagne. They'd drank it. He'd kissed her and one thing had led to another. He'd bitten her, but she'd asked him to. If she had any other drugs in her system, she'd taken them on her own.

The thing he didn't mention was that he'd had a little extra help besides champagne and his stunning good looks. Not many people knew that some vampires did have extra...abilities. Erickson, and his younger brother, could be quite persuasive when they wanted to be. It never left a trace, so there was no way to prove that Erickson had done anything. No physical evidence anyway. Shianne, however, knew the whole truth. She'd been outside the door when Tedi had come staggering out after the tryst. She knew that Erickson had used his abilities to get what he wanted.

Erickson had convinced Ibrahim to let him tell his father and Di, and the lawyer had agreed. Instead of going to Di, however, he'd gone to his sister and told her everything. Now, the two of them were trying to figure out the best time to break the news to their father. Neither one were dumb enough to tell Di first.

"How much time did Ibrahim give before he called Dad directly?" Shianne asked for what seemed like the hundredth time.

It said something about how rattled Erickson was that he didn't sound annoyed when he answered the same thing he'd answered every time before. "Until Dad and Alexander meet us in Santorini. He understood that I wanted to tell Dad face-to-face."

Shianne nodded. "We don't even know for sure it's yours, Erickson." The words sounded just as empty as they had the first dozen times she'd said it.

When Erickson looked up at her, there was a look on his face she'd never seen her brother wear. Panic. "But what if it is?"

"Then we'll deal with it," she said firmly.

"Deal with what?"

Shianne and Erickson both froze, their bodies taking on that stillness that most natural vampires seemed to have inherently. Out of the corner of her eye, Shianne saw Di step into the room and her brain scrambled to find something that she could say.

"If Erickson's fangs set off the metal detectors at the airport," she blurted out the sentence.

Di raised an eyebrow. "We're not going through metal detectors, Shianne. The network chartered private jets, and if we weren't taking them, we'd be taking our own."

"Oh, right." Shianne tried to look embarrassed. She really hoped her reputation as a dumb blond was enough to convince Di.

"I told her that too, but she wouldn't listen." Erickson joined in the lie.

Di's eyes narrowed and she looked from one to the other. Shianne fought to keep her face blank, her eyes wide and innocent. It must have worked because, Di finally made a dismissive gesture with her hand. "We don't have time for this. Are you two packed?"

"Yes," they chorused together.

"Then get your stuff downstairs. Just because the planes are waiting on us doesn't mean we aren't keeping to a schedule." She turned and walked out without another word.

When she was sure Di was far enough away not to hear her,

Shianne let out a rush of air. She looked at her brother and saw her own emotions mirrored back at her. Relief at having gotten away with the lie. Anxiety over what would come next. One thing was for sure, no matter what happened, things would never be the same.

CHAPTER FIVE

The hotel room was one of the nicest in London, complete with an amazing view of the city, a king-sized bed with thousand thread-count sheets, and a massive bathtub that could hold at least three people. It was the perfect room for a honeymoon or a romantic getaway. Or the perfect place to bring a conquest or two. A short while ago, that's exactly what Alexander Vamp would've been doing. After four nights in London, he should've bedded at least half a dozen handsome Brits. Instead, he was lying in the huge bed – alone.

Alexander stared up at the ceiling, his normally bright green eyes dull, his medium length dirty blond hair a tangled mess. He'd been awake for hours but hadn't moved yet. He knew he should be getting up, showering, getting dressed, getting something to eat. He just couldn't muster up enough energy to do anything more than wallow. His father would be by soon with one of the feeders they'd selected while in the city and he knew he'd have to force himself to eat. His already slender frame was thinner than it had ever been thanks to his loss of appetite for the past two months, and he knew that if he wasn't careful, Heir would think Alexander was suffering from an eating disorder like his sister.

It wasn't vanity or a need for control responsible for the middle Vamp son's lack of interest in food – or anything else for that matter. He'd been trying to play it off as exhaustion since he'd been busy designing for his 'Forever Twink' underwear line, but it wasn't that either. And the same thing that was keeping him from sleeping and eating and having sex was also keeping him from drawing. Oh, he could still draw, but every time he picked up a pencil and a pad of paper, the same image flowed from his fingers. The image of the reason for his depression.

Noah French, an eighteen-year-old human. Granted, he had one of those faces too pretty for a guy, beautiful blond hair, gorgeous blue eyes and a body meant to be admired. He was one of the most singularly attractive men Alexander had ever seen, and he'd been checking out the male members of the species since the mid-eighteen hundreds. But he was still human. Mortal. Aging – something Alexander hadn't done for more than six centuries. The Vamps spent their time among humans, slept with them, sometimes even befriended them, but they all knew not to get too attached. Time moved slowly for vampires and falling for a human was just asking for a broken heart.

He'd told himself that a million times, but it didn't change anything. In the first couple weeks after he'd screwed things up with Noah, he'd tried to go back to his old ways. He gone to clubs and brought home the prettiest boys, ones who would keep getting carded well into their late twenties. He'd challenged himself to seduce men who claimed to be straight and succeeded every time. He'd slept with athletes and musicians, brooding poets and self-absorbed actors. He'd gorged himself on sex until he'd woken up one morning with two men in his bed and another two curled up on the floor, and realized that he didn't want it anymore. He didn't want the empty, meaningless rutting of two bodies, or more as was often the case with him. He'd sent the men on their way and that had been the last time anyone had shared his bed.

He'd been forced to admit it to himself then. He didn't want anyone in his bed but Noah. And it wasn't just the sex he missed, though that had been amazing. He missed Noah's quiet strength. His unwavering belief that Alexander was more than just the flaky middle-son Vamp who went from one insane venture to the next. When Noah had looked at him with those steady blue eyes, Alexander had believed he could accomplish anything.

And now that was gone.

At least, it was gone in real life. In the media, however, Alexander and Noah were the new power couple representing the LGBT community. Gregory Firth, the PR agent who represented Alexander and Taylor Ann, had been quite insistent that appearances be kept, particularly since the show hadn't yet aired the episodes where Alexander had blown it all to hell.

Alexander and Noah had only spoken once since the last

incident and it had been shortly after Taylor Ann's meltdown during the premiere ball. Gregory had used their busy schedules to explain why they weren't spending time together, but the tabloids had started speculating just a few weeks ago. Not that Alexander had been following any of the stories. No, Pru was the entertainment news junkie when it came to stories about the Vamps and she'd kept Alexander informed on all of the latest.

And the latest was, while Alexander was out of the country, Noah had become a New York paparazzi darling, or whatever a person who hated being stalked by reporters was called. They followed him everywhere, Pru said, commenting on what he was wearing and drinking and how he looked at everyone around him. At first, it had been just the men, fueling rumors that there was trouble in paradise, but then, over the past few days, pictures had been cropping up of Noah with various women and the captions had wondered if Noah wasn't just straying from Alexander, but from his sexuality as well. At least that part wasn't something Alexander believed.

He sighed and rolled out of bed, heading for the bathroom. Today was his premiere and he couldn't call off with a case of broken heart. He had to prove to everyone that he wasn't a screw up, that he could be every bit as successful as his older brother. To do that, he first needed to be presentable, and that meant a shower...and clothes.

****

Heir knew that something was wrong with his usually carefree son but couldn't get a straight answer. Whenever he asked Alexander about it, the boy would lie and say that he was just tired. Alexander had never been a very good liar, at least not to his father. It bothered Heir that he wasn't able to determine the cause of Alexander's moodiness over the past few months, but he'd had so much else on his mind that it had been impossible for him to focus on one singular problem.

The most pressing matter, of course, was the season two excursion. Heir hadn't left the United States for more than a business day trip since he'd first stepped foot onto the soil. Di had returned to the old country on occasion during their first few decades in America, but even she had grown attached to their life here. Over the years he'd kept his family safe in the States and now they were heading right back to the places he didn't want to go. London was relatively safe, but that wasn't their true destination. After the show tonight, he and Alexander would be leaving to meet the others on the Greek Isle of Santorini where they would visit with his mother, Rupa, and this was the reason for his concern.

His children knew the stories he and Di had told them about where they came from, about their family. They didn't know the vast number of stories left untold, though he knew Leo suspected, and therein was the problem. The others would enjoy themselves and be easily steered away from conversations that could lead to uncomfortable questions. Leo, however, had inherited his mother's tenacious personality, and would not be content to be escorted around. He would search. He would ask questions, and if he found answers, things could become very bad, very fast.

This was his own fault, Heir knew. He'd chosen to allow a television network to film his family, and he hadn't thought to tell his lawyer to make sure no travel arrangements could be made without his consent. At least he knew it wouldn't happen again. After the death of the network head, Hiram Whet, Heir had met with the new network head, Wendy McMillan, and negotiated a new contract with the stipulation that the network never again make decisions regarding his family. He'd been a bit harsher than he generally liked to be, but he'd also gotten the job done and found out a bit of information that made him think less critically of the late Hiram. Wendy had informed Heir that the studio had based their decision on what viewers seemed to want rather than what the network president had wanted. Hiram had, in fact, argued against making the decision without consulting Heir. It hadn't made this any better, but at least Heir knew now that Hiram had been a decent human.

Heir glanced at his phone. Di would be calling shortly to give him a progress report. The family should be mid-flight if they left at the time Di had planned, and Heir never doubted his right hand's ability to get things done on time. Aside from wanting to make sure that his family was doing well, Di would also be reporting on Leo. The youngest Vamp son would need to be watched carefully during this entire trip. Heir could not allow the boy to stumble on certain truths. It was far too dangerous.

Heir sighed. He needed to take the feeder to Alexander. He could've just sent the man over, but Leo wasn't the only one who needed to be watched. Heir wasn't about to let another child starve themselves. He would take the feeder and stay until Alexander ate. Then they would go to the venue of the fashion show and make all of the final arrangements for the premiere that evening. There was much to do, and for that Heir was grateful. The more he had to do, the less time he had to think about how unprepared he was for what was to come.

CHAPTER SIX

Shianne had forgotten how beautiful Santorini was at the end of the dry season. It wasn't too hot, but the November rains hadn't yet brought the winter chill with them. The clouds had come, however, and that allowed the Vamps to be out and about with just regular umbrellas to shield them in the moments the clouds broke. They didn't have to try to manage the big ugly things that Di had brought, just in case, and Shianne was totally grateful for that. She may have needed her cute little dress to cover more up top than normal, but she still didn't want to hide her figure. The last time she'd been here, she'd been Pru's age, old enough to be interested in all the hotness of Greek men, but far too young to do anything about it. Now, she fully intended to bask in their admiration.

As she followed Di up the steps, Shianne turned her arm this way and that, admiring the way her tanned skin looked against the white walls. The steps under her high heels were white too, limestone placed a little too evenly to be natural, but so long ago that they appeared to have been hewn from the ground. Rupa had lived at the edge of Oia for centuries and had done little to modernize her estate.

A breeze blew in across the Aegean Sea and Shianne turned her face into it, breathing in deep the clean air. One of the disadvantages to having the enhanced senses of a vampire was how much worse big cities smelled. Shianne smiled as she looked out over bright blue water. She understood why her grandmother had chosen this place. For a brief moment, she saw herself joining Rupa here, leaving behind all of the hustle and bustle of the cities the Vamps called home. No more paparazzi, no family drama, just the peace and solitude of the island. She sighed. She really hoped she wasn't becoming maudlin. Her siblings provided enough angst for the family.

"Grandmother!!" Prussia pushed past Shianne, nearly knocking her off her feet. The youngest Vamp didn't even pause as she bounded up the stairs, her fiery hair streaming out behind her in its ever-present ponytail.

Shianne bit back the growl she wanted to send her sister's way. The CDW cameraman was right behind her and Shianne knew that her father wouldn't be happy if one of the first images of the Vamp family in Greece was of Shianne snapping at her little sister. At least the littlest Vamp was wearing a nice pair of jeans and a blouse that wasn't ripped or stained. Shianne forced a smile and kept walking, focusing on her grandmother.

Rupa had, like her son, Settled when she was older. In her mid-seventies, she was still beautiful, with an elegance that Shianne had always associated with the glamorous movies stars of the Hollywood Golden Age. She dressed simply in a long, pale green dress that Shianne knew was far more expensive than it looked. Like Heir, Rupa had done well for herself over the centuries.

It wasn't until she was level with her grandmother that Shianne realized the vampire wasn't alone under the blue canopy that sheltered her from the sun. Standing to the side and just behind Rupa was a human who Shianne immediately thought was as close to a Greek god as a man could be. Thick black curls, eyes such a deep shade of brown that if she hadn't had vampire sight, Shianne would've thought they were black as well. His face was classically handsome, like something Michelangelo would have sculpted. And that body...he was wearing shorts and a white, short-sleeved, button-up shirt, both tailored perfectly to show off his broad shoulders, muscular chest and narrow waist.

"Hello, there." Shianne smiled at him as her grandmother greeted Di.

"Hello." His accent was thick and it was clear from his expression that he wasn't comfortable speaking English.

That was okay. He didn't need to be able to speak to look pretty.

"Shianne, my darling girl." Rupa held open her arms and Shianne stepped into them.

After a moment, Shianne stepped back. She'd almost forgotten how much she loved her grandmother. It had been so long. "You're looking beautiful, as always."

Rupa smiled, her hazel eyes sparkling. "Thank you, my dear. And you have become quite a beautiful woman yourself."

Shianne couldn't resist shooting a glance at the stone-faced man behind them. "May I ask who he is?"

"Ah, yes." Rupa straightened to include the entire group in the introduction. "This is Aris, my assistant." Her eyes flicked to the camera crew, fast enough that none of the humans would have seen. She added in Greek, "And my feeder."

Di smiled and nodded before turning and speaking to Aris in his native tongue, telling him that she was pleased to meet him. Shianne may not have remembered how to speak much in Greek, but she still understood a decent amount.

"Boss ain't gonna like it if they keep talking gibberish like that." One of the new crew members spoke in what Shianne assumed was supposed to be a hushed tone. Unfortunately for him, it wasn't quiet enough for the vampires not to hear.

"Excuse me?" Di spun around, the look on her face fierce enough that even Shianne took a step back. Di's eyes flashed as she started down the stairs to where the white-faced young man was standing. Dr. Darcy nearly fell backwards down a step in his desire to be away from the vampire. "Your name?"

"Franklin Gumble." His voice was shaking and Shianne didn't blame him. Lesser men than him had wet themselves when Di given them that look.

"You may return to the airport, Mr. Gumble. I will call your employer to inform them that they will need to arrange for a return ticket for you. You are no longer welcome to film my family."

"But – I – "

"Think very carefully before you speak, Mr. Gumble," Di said. "And bear in mind that my patience with your ignorance is wearing thin."

The man's mouth opened and closed twice, then his shoulders slumped and he turned, walking back down the stairs.

Di surveyed the rest of the crew with flashing eyes. "Does anyone else have a problem with the way we're speaking?" Heads shook in unison. Apparently satisfied, Di turned and walked back up to where Rupa was waiting. "I'm sorry about that," she apologized.

"It is quite all right," Rupa said. She waved a hand dismissively. "Shall we go inside?"

As the vampires and Aris headed for the sprawling house, Shianne fell in step on one side of her grandmother, Leo on the other.

"So, Grandmother," Shianne couldn't resist a little teasing. "Where'd you find the man-toy?"

Rupa gave Shianne a sideways look of exasperation, but Shianne could see a hint of a smile. Rupa may have seemed like she was all old-fashioned, but Shianne knew she'd gotten at least a bit of her wild streak from that side of the family.

Leo, on the other hand, didn't appreciate the comment. "Shianne, I do not believe our father would appreciate your implication that Aris is anything other than a feeder."

Shianne grinned. She knew she should leave it be, but Leo was just too much fun to pick at. "Does that mean he's single?"

****

Pru rolled her eyes at her eldest sister's comment. Only Shianne. Even as she thought it, she frowned. That wasn't right. It wasn't only Shianne who would say something like that. Erickson would usually be right there with her. He may have been the family's public business face and behaved himself in public, but all of the Vamps knew that he and Shianne generally kept up their own running commentary.

She looked around. Where was her brother? She'd barely seen him over the past couple days and, now that she thought about it, hadn't even noticed him on the plane ride. That was weird. Erickson was always at the center of attention. It was another way he and Shianne were alike. As much as Leo, and even Taylor Ann, avoided the spotlight, the two oldest Vamps couldn't seem to get enough of it. Being quiet and out of the way wasn't like Erickson at all. Pru hadn't bothered following any stories about her two oldest siblings in at least two months. There were way too many of them. Besides, she'd been focusing on someone else than Alexander.

When she finally spotted Erickson trudging along behind Taylor Ann, Pru actually felt a little worried. If he was human, she would've said he looked sick. She thought about going over and asking him what was wrong, but as soon as they entered their grandmother's house, he caught up to Rupa and began talking. She pulled out her phone. Maybe Alexander would know what was going on.

"Excuse, please."

Pru jumped, startled. She hadn't realized that she'd stopped walking right in front of Aris. "Oh, sorry." She took a step to the side and let the human pass.

She looked down at her phone and sighed. No, Alexander wouldn't know why Erickson was acting so odd because Alexander hadn't been paying much attention to anything except the articles on Noah that Pru had been bringing to him. She'd liked her brother's human, but she couldn't say it really surprised her that the relationship had ended badly. She loved Alexander, but she wasn't sure a monogamous relationship was something he could handle. He'd really have to be in love for him to change the way he'd lived his life for centuries.

An idea popped into her head and she grinned. What her brother needed was a pick-me-up, something to get his mind off of Noah. What better distraction was there than a guy even she thought was hot? She snapped a photo of Aris and quickly sent it off to Alexander. She considered taking one of Taylor Ann's therapist, Stephen, too, but he was lean and blond, too close to what Noah looked like. Aris was completely different, and that was good. That was one brother taken care of. Now she just had to figure out what was up with Erickson and how she could fix it.

CHAPTER SEVEN

Alexander checked his reflection for what seemed like the thousandth time. His hands were shaking as he smoothed down his hair, the movement so minuscule that only Heir noticed. Heir put his hand on his son's shoulder as they waited for the elevator. He hadn't seen Alexander this nervous in decades. A surge of pride went through him. He had never seen his son throw himself into any activity as he had these past few months.

Heir frowned as Alexander shifted his weight from one foot to the other. He could feel the Vamp's bones beneath his skin. Alexander had always been slender; he'd taken after Treasa that way. This, however, was more than just his normal lean build. He had lost more weight than Heir had realized. Perhaps this vacation was exactly what he needed. The stress of starting a clothing line was more than most people realized. Heir himself had experienced loss of appetite and insomnia when he first opened House of Vamp, and he'd been far older than Alexander.

"You have done an excellent job getting things ready for tonight, Alexander," Heir said. "Relax and be your usual charming self. Everyone will love your work."

Alexander glanced over his shoulder and gave Heir a smile that looked forced. "Thank you."

Heir dropped his hand, his eyes staying on Alexander as the elevator doors opened and his son walked inside. Heir studied the boy's face, seeing now the extra paleness of his skin, the slight prominence of his cheekbones. Vampires didn't get sick from germs, but they could make themselves weaker through starvation. Taylor Ann had been proof of that. Heir truly hoped that the fashion world hadn't caused another of his children to succumb to its latest obsession with body image. He would keep an eye on Alexander, he decided, and make certain that it was only stress causing these changes. He would not let what happened to his middle daughter happen again.

****

Alexander knew that his father was concerned and he hoped that the assumption would be stress. Technically, he supposed it was, just not because of tonight's show. Alexander's nerves were stretched taut, every cell in his body humming with anxiety and eagerness, and all because he'd made a call to the agency supplying the night's models and insisted that one specific eighteen year-old be included.

As he and his father stepped off of the elevators and into the corridor, he tried to portray the cool, aloof demeanor Erickson had always given off when attending black carpet events – for the Vamps it was always black carpet, as if red would make them think of food – but he didn't think he was pulling it off. His heart was beating faster than normal, almost as fast as a human's, and he could hear how ragged his breathing was. He rubbed his sweating palms on his pants in an attempt to dry them. He didn't want his hands to be damp when he finally saw...him. Even though he knew he should be thinking about the show and all of the people he was getting ready to meet, all he could think about was spotting Noah.

His phone buzzed and he pulled it out of his pocket. "Incoming photo from Pru." He was suddenly very glad he'd turned his ringer off. Pru had set her ring and text tone to a Meredith Brooks song from the nineties and the lyrics were hardly appropriate for a public setting.

He smiled fondly at the thought of his little sister, but didn't bother to check the message. If Pru was sending pictures from Greece, he felt it was a pretty safe bet that they were going to be of random men. She'd been worried about him ever since Noah had left. Not that she'd come out and said it. That wasn't Pru's style. She came across as the typical rebellious tween who didn't like anything or anyone, but he knew that she was actually the one who felt things the deepest. Growing up, aging, the way they did wasn't easy, but it had been even more difficult for Pru and Leo. They'd been so young when their mother had died, and the sudden loss had devastated the family for so long, that Alexander knew it'd had a profound impact on them both. Leo had turned inward, building up a wall as he searched for answers to questions he seemed to think would make a difference. Pru had done the opposite, letting her negative emotions shield her from being hurt. Out of all of the siblings, Pru was closest to him, and even he rarely got a glimpse of what was truly going on in her head.

"Alexander."

Heir's tone said that he'd had to repeat his son's name.

"Sorry." Alexander gave his father and the two men in front of him a charming smile. "Got a little distracted there."

"It's not like you don't have a reason to have your mind elsewhere." The taller of the two men spoke with a crisp British accent as he put out his hand, his dark eyes twinkling. Alexander shook it, forcing himself not to pull back when the man's hand lingered just a bit too long. "To be so successful, so young, it's a blessing and a curse."

Alexander recognized the man now. Lincoln Childs, one of London's biggest playboys. His reputation rivaled both Erickson's and Alexander's since Lincoln was equally 'friendly' with both genders. He'd hit it big as a pop star when he was just fifteen and by seventeen had been in and out of rehab three times. He'd finally cleaned up by twenty and was now twenty-five and managing his own recording label.

"Thank you," Alexander said politely. He didn't want to give Lincoln the wrong idea. A few months ago, he probably would've put the handsome young man on his 'to do' list, but that was before.

"Welcome to London," the other man spoke up. He had a thicker accent and a scruffy beard covering most of his face. "Been here before?"

"It's been a while," Alexander said with a smile. "Thank you, Mr. Coulson." He didn't need an introduction to the lead singer of Dead in the Water, a Scottish band with a reputation for being a bit on the crazy side. He'd attended one of their concerts once when they'd first started out and had spent three days partying with them in their hotel suite. He wasn't surprised Coulson didn't remember him. Back then, Alexander had dyed his hair black, and been wearing eyeliner and leather, just to see if he'd like the scene. It had been fun for a couple weeks, but even hot guys in tight leather weren't worth the effort of keeping his hair dyed and putting on eyeliner. Somehow, Alexander doubted that his father would appreciate him bringing up his past encounter with the band, so he posed for a picture with the two men and kept moving.

"Alexander, this is Mrs. Robertson," Heir said as they approached a tall, thin woman in her mid-fifties.

She held out a hand, palm down, the gesture clearly saying that she was expecting something more genteel than a handshake. Fortunately, Alexander had grown up in a time where that had still been the norm, particularly in the high class circles. Heir might not have traveled much outside of the United States after moving there, but Alexander, Erickson, Val, Shianne and Taylor Ann had all done a tour of Europe, Britain and the British colonies in the late eighteen hundreds.

He took her hand and bowed over it, pressing his lips against her dry skin. As he straightened, he caught the heat in her eyes that meant she was mentally undressing him. That was fine, as long as it didn't pass from mental to outright seduction. He didn't mind dancing and friendly flirtation with the opposite sex, but when they tried to take it further, it always annoyed him, and he wasn't sure he had much patience for it tonight.

"So, Alexander, are you the sort of designer who models his clothes, or do you only leave that to others?" Mrs. Robertson sidled closer. "Because I would be very interested in a private show."

Before either Alexander or Heir could respond, another voice interrupted.

"Are you giving private shows now, Alexander?" A male voice came from their left.

Three sets of eyes turned to see a statuesque figure in one of last season's corsets, a flared skirt and thigh-high red leather heeled boots sauntering towards them. Lashes so thick and long they had to be fake surrounded bright blue eyes and a long blond wig completed the outfit.

"Hey, Devyn." Alexander grinned. He'd met the cross-dressing actor a few years back at a Hollywood premiere. Devyn had been in the movie and Alexander had been 'dating' a few of the guys on the set. One of them had snagged tickets.

"Rena, I think your husband was looking for you." Devyn pointed towards an older man standing a few yards away. "Might want to get to it before he scampers off with another of those bimbos who're always hanging on him."

Alexander waited until Mrs. Robertson left before laughing and hugging Devyn. The knot in his chest had eased some. He didn't see Devyn often enough to consider him a close friend, but the two of them had hit it off and always made a point of at least going out for drinks when they were in the same place. The best part was that neither of them had ever harbored any sort of romantic or lustful feelings for the other. It was pure friendship.

"Dad, this is Devyn Belle."

Heir held out his hand and Devyn shook it. "Nice to meet you, Mr. Vamp."

"Just Heir, please."

As his father made polite small talk following the greeting, Alexander looked around again for Noah. Surely the agency hadn't decided not to do as he'd asked and send someone else. Unless, Alexander thought suddenly, Noah had refused to come. It was a possibility. Granted, Noah had a contract, but with him being as popular right now as he was, Alexander didn't think the agency would press it if Noah was adamant.

Suddenly, Alexander was sure that Noah was here. He could feel someone staring at him. There was a difference between someone looking at him because this was his show, or even the stares he got from fans. He could feel someone's gaze boring into him, willing him to look at them. He turned, expecting to see blond hair and blue eyes, but instead saw thick sandy curls and eyes so dark brown that they almost looked black. The face was strong, angular, handsome, but not pretty. He was tall and muscular, probably a good six inches taller and eighty pounds heavier than Alexander's slender five foot, nine inch frame, but Alexander didn't mind that. In fact, if circumstances had been different, he might've walked over to the man boldly ogling him and kissed him, just to see what happened.

"Mason Kries has been blogging about this all week," Devyn said in Alexander's ear. "But I don't think he's here for just the clothes."

Alexander deliberately turned his back to Mason without acknowledging that he'd seen the other man. He shoved his hands into his pockets. "Well, he'll be disappointed then."

"So it is true?" Devyn teased. "The great Alexander Vamp, seducer of straight men and lover of many has decided he's finally found 'the one'?"

Before Alexander had to figure out how to answer the question, Heir approached with another pair of celebrities who wanted to have their picture taken with Alexander. They kept coming, one after another, barely giving Alexander time to process, much less think of anything else. By the time the last of them left to find their seats, it was almost time for the show to begin and only Heir and Alexander remained outside the venue with the security guards.

A sharp intake of breath told him that someone else had just stepped into the hallway.

Heir's eyes flicked behind them, then back to Alexander. "I'll make sure our seats are ready," he said. "You don't have long."

Alexander nodded and waited until his father was almost to the doors before he turned, his stomach twisting as he finally saw the one person he'd been looking for.

Noah was here.

CHAPTER EIGHT

Leo found himself alone as he slowly walked through his grandmother's house. He could see the progression of the architecture through the years, though it stopped sometime in the sixteen hundreds. He admired that about Rupa. She, he thought, was a perfect blend of the modern and the ancient, taking that which was beneficial from the new world, but never losing her grasp on the old.

Aris, for example, was a prime example. The Vamps had staff from whom they fed, but it was a delicate subject. They were butlers and maids, cooks and drivers. While Rupa gave the impression of conforming to societal norms, she had not flinched at introducing Aris as her feeder to the family. Should she have come to one of the Vamps homes in America, the staff would have been introduced by name and position, their feeder status only discussed when it was time to eat.

Finally, he spotted what he'd been hoping to find: a half-open door through which he could see books. He smiled, and for once it was not only because he preferred to be alone. If anyone he knew had books older than those his father owned, it would be his grandmother. He did not know if he would find what he was looking for here, but it was a better place to start than the redacted libraries in the American houses. Heir had removed almost everything that could have led Leo to the truth. Not the truth about the origins of their species. That had once been his obsession, and he had been certain that it would give him a reason, a rationale, behind his mother's death, but some months ago, he had found something that his father had not removed from the library, and it had changed everything. He touched his pocket, but did not remove the papers. He had made it this far without them being discovered. It would not do to lose them now.

He looked up and down the hall to ensure that none of the camera crew had followed him. He had doubted they would. They were concerned with the mundane affairs of human entertainment, the prattling about gossip and fashion, the drama of family squabbles. They wanted to see Erickson and Shianne talk about parties and liaisons. They wanted to see Pru do something impulsive and foolish. They wanted break-downs and break-ups. He offered none of those things and so they let him be.

Leo shook his head as he carefully closed the door behind him. Sometimes he felt sorry for the humans, with their short lives, so consumed by the fleeting and unimportant.

He looked around the room. This room was close to the same

size as the library in Boston, though it had fewer books. Back home, Heir had filled his libraries with more than history and philosophy. He had allowed popular literature and classics to be brought in over the years, the first often turning to the latter with the passage of time. Heir had mistakenly hoped, Leo assumed, that these would encourage the others to read. Rupa, it appeared, had not added a single volume in the last century and a half, perhaps longer. A desk sat in the center of the room, both it and the matching chair looking to be at least three, if not four, hundred years old. A dozen or so paintings, some as old as the desk, lined the walls and various sculptures and other historical artifacts sat scattered around the room. Rupa had more art work than her son did.

Leo leaned back against the door to ensure that no one would be able to enter without him knowing, and only then did he reach into his jacket pocket and remove the soft leather pouch in which he had hidden the papers he had found. They were fragile, yellowed with age, and written in a language Leo could not decipher. He had spent nearly every opportunity he had since finding them trying to make sense of the markings on the pages, but without success. He had made copies of the pages and hidden them in each of the houses in America, as well as bringing two copies with him, but he carried the originals nonetheless. They carried the proof that something about his mother's death was being hidden from him.

He did not unfold the pages, but simply looked at the mark. He did not know if it was a symbol of a group, a singular person or a place. It could, he supposed, even be symbolic of an event or a signal to action. All he knew was that he had seen it one other place and the image was burned into his mind just as the mark had been burned into his mother's flesh. His father had dismissed his questions about it as if saying that Leo had imagined the whole thing, but these papers were proof that he had not, and that either Heir or Di – or both – knew more than they had said.

This symbol was where he would begin, he decided. Somewhere in this room, one of these books or artifacts must contain an identification or origin of the mark. He put the papers back into his pocket and stepped away from the door, eager to get started.

He had only skimmed the titles on two shelves when the door opened. He looked over, fully expecting to see one of those invasive cameras, but it was his grandmother who was entering. He smiled at her, "Grandmother."

"Leonardo." She smiled back, her eyes twinkling. "I knew that I would find you here, among the books." She held out her hand. "Come. I wish to hear stories of your lives in America. Your sisters and brother are gathering in the garden. Please join us."

He wanted to refuse and remain here. He had waited so long and he could feel that the answer was here, just within his grasp. Instead, he took his grandmother's hand.

"Of course," he said, allowing her to lead him from the library. Perhaps, he thought, he could speak with her about his discovery. She, after all, was the oldest vampire he knew. He would have to be careful with his questions, however. He was not sure if his father was the only one who was keeping secrets and he would not want to tip his hand. He would tread lightly and hope that his feet took him in the correct direction.

CHAPTER NINE

It was as if all of the air had rushed out of the room. He stopped breathing, stopped blinking, sure that if he did either one, everything would come rushing back and *he* would be gone.

Noah's eyes met his and Alexander felt his stomach flip, his heart give two heavy, hard thumps against his ribcage. Sound and air came back, rushing into his ears and lungs so suddenly that he gasped. He had to force himself to match his pace to Noah's maddeningly slow one when all he wanted to do was use the bit of extra speed all vampires had – nothing like the blurs in movies and television, but still faster than a human – and run to him. He wanted to pick Noah up in his arms, kiss him until neither one of them could breathe. Instead, he settled for an awkward smile and an extra bounce in his step when Noah returned it. Granted, it wasn't the full, joyful curve of those luscious lips that Alexander had wanted, but it at least wasn't a scowl or a frown, or worse, indifference.

"You came." He mentally kicked himself for stating the obvious.

Noah nodded. "I don't have much time before I have to get backstage, but I wanted to come thank you for requesting me for the show."

"Of course," Alexander said. He wanted to add that if it hadn't been for Noah, there wouldn't have been a show. The human was his muse. With Noah's beautiful face and lean, sculpted body, he could've been the muse for a thousand artists.

"How's Taylor Ann?"

The question surprised him only because he'd thought Noah would ask about him first. That was a bit selfish, Alexander supposed. After all, Taylor Ann had been more ill than any of them had realized. "She's doing really well," he said. "She has a counselor, Stephen, who's working wonders with her. He's amazing."

Noah's mouth flattened and Alexander instantly realized his mistake.

"I mean, the way he is with her and everything." He hurried to try to rectify the situation before Noah really thought that he was sleeping with his sister's therapist. "She's actually been eating with us again. Not a lot, but enough. She's put on weight and looks good. I don't think she could've done it without him." Alexander was vaguely aware that he was babbling.

"What about Pru?" Noah cut in, his voice quiet, his face blank. "Some of the reporters who've been stalking me said that Karson kid broke up with her."

Alexander shook his head, forcing himself to focus on the question. "They weren't really together," he said. "They're still really good friends."

"That's good," Noah said. "It's not always possible to stay friends with someone after..." His voice trailed off and he looked away.

The silence that followed was more awkward than anything Alexander had experienced before. Sure, he'd had awkward encounters with some of his many dalliances over the years, but those had generally resulted in him making a quick getaway, at times to avoid accusations from angry wives or girlfriends. He didn't want to walk away now. He wanted to find a way to fix this before it was too late.

"Well." Noah broke the silence. "I need to go get ready. I'm walking first, middle and last."

Alexander felt a swell of pride. He hadn't told the agency anything about where to place Noah. The human had earned the spotlight all on his own.

"Um, bye." Noah turned abruptly and walked away.

Pride immediately turned into disappointment. He'd really been hoping that he could at least get some encouragement, something that would tell him that all wasn't lost. Instead, he was even more at a loss as to where he stood with Noah than he had been before they'd talked. Gregory had called Alexander before he and Heir had left for London and had given specific instructions regarding keeping up appearances. Any men Alexander took to bed, he was supposed to be discreet and make sure they signed a non-disclosure agreement. Alexander had scoffed, but agreed. He'd known it wouldn't be necessary. Another of Gregory's instructions, however, had been to make sure that Noah would continue to go along with the charade. They were supposed to be seen together if they were at the same event, and seen laughing, talking, holding hands. Under no circumstances were they to do anything to alert the media that they weren't together anymore. If Noah wanted to go public with the break-up, Gregory wanted to make an official statement first.

Alexander ran his hand through his hair and sighed. He'd have to find Noah after the show and tell him all of this. He hadn't wanted to be so blunt, but it looked like that would be the only way he'd get answers. He turned toward the doors, knowing he needed to be inside, playing his part, but his heart wasn't in it. This had been his dream, having a successful business venture that he enjoyed. Something that made his father proud. Now, all he could think about was Noah. He sighed again. What had he been thinking, falling for a human?

****

Noah stopped just inside the dressing room and leaned back against the wall, closing his eyes against the tears that wanted to come. Why had he done that? He'd known it hadn't been a good idea to see Alexander, but he'd gone anyway. He'd lied to himself, saying that he just wanted to thank Alexander for not blackballing him when it would've been easy to do with the Vamps' connections. He really had wanted to know how Taylor Ann and Pru were doing, too. All of that, he knew, could've been done over the phone.

He'd wanted to see Alexander, he finally admitted. It didn't matter that two months had passed and he was trying to move on with his life. He was drawn to the vampire in a way he'd never been drawn to anyone else before. If he hadn't known better, he would've said that Alexander had enthralled him, or that there'd been some sort of weird almost sire-bond thing going on between them, but he knew better. That wasn't how things worked. That wasn't how Alexander worked.

It was just who he was. His face and his body. His soul. The way those bright green eyes would light up when he saw someone or something he cared about: Pru, a beautiful painting...Noah. Then there was the whole other part of Alexander that no one else saw. The vulnerable Vamp who never thought he'd be as good or special as his big brother. The one who was so special, had so much potential inside him that Noah couldn't understand how no one else could see it. And they didn't, not really. Pru did, Noah amended. And Taylor Ann to some extent. He supposed that was why he liked those two the best out of the rest of the Vamps.

Noah swore and pushed himself away from the wall. He rubbed the backs of his hands across his eyes and set his jaw. No. He wasn't going to do this. He'd cried enough tears over Alexander

Vamp. He wasn't going to let one little encounter ruin all of the progress he'd made.

"Noah!"

Someone called his name and he remembered that he had to get ready. That was good, he thought. Something to keep his mind off of Alexander.

Now, if he could just keep himself from looking in the audience each time he went down the catwalk to see if he could find the vampire among the humans.

****

The show was a smashing success. At least, that's what everyone was telling him. Alexander only remembered three things from the entire line-up: the white boxer briefs Noah had worn, the bright red briefs that had reminded him of what was underneath and the itty-bitty black briefs that had been almost too small to be considered decent. The rest was all a blur of trying to resist the nearly overwhelming impulse to jump on stage and have his way with Noah right then and there. Of course, that was ludicrous and Alexander had much better self-control than that, but the R-rated images refused to go away.

By the time the show was done, Alexander's hands were curled into fists and it was all he could do to smile at his father's praise for a job well-done.

"Are you feeling well, Alexander?" Heir asked, new concern on his face. "You look as if you are going to be ill?"

"I'm fine, thank you," Alexander said tightly. He stood as he caught a glimpse of blond hair weaving through the crowd. "But I haven't eaten much these past few days." He kept his voice low, not wanting any of the people heading his way to overhear him. "I think I may need to feed."

"Ah, of course," Heir nodded.

The family patriarch was adept at concealing what he was feeling, so the fact that Alexander caught a glimpse of relief meant that his father really had been worried. Alexander felt bad that he'd worried his dad, but the best way to make that better was to let Heir think that he was going to eat. Besides, Alexander reasoned as he excused himself, if he could get Noah to talk to him, maybe it would make things better.

He kept a polite, but strained smile on his face as he made his way through the crowd of admirers, hoping that his expression would lend to a rumor of him feeling ill. Not that vampires got sick, but that wasn't exactly common knowledge. He gave excuses to some as he passed, barely hearing the words coming out of his mouth, counting on his innate ability to charm to make himself seem apologetic rather than rude. His eyes stayed fixed on the exit. When he saw the doors open, he moved faster. If Noah left, Alexander knew he'd lose him forever. It was an irrational fear, he knew, but that didn't stop the panic from spreading.

He was almost to the exit when he collided with something solid and nice-smelling.

"I was hoping to run into you, though I wasn't expecting it to be literal."

Alexander looked up at the sound of a deep voice in his ear. At first, all he saw were pools of near black, then he registered the rest. It was the blogger who'd been checking him out earlier.

"I'm sorry," he muttered as he disentangled himself. "I have to go see someone."

He thought Mason said something to him, but he didn't stop to ask for a repeat. Whatever it was, it didn't matter. All that mattered was getting through those doors.

"Noah!" The name was on his lips and spilling over even before he finished stepping into the hallway. Even as his brain registered what he was seeing, he walked another half dozen steps, then stopped.

All of the excitement and anxiety of the day drained away, taking every last drop of hope with it until he was empty and numb.

Noah slowly turned towards him and the gorgeous model holding his hand turned as well. Noah's eyes widened slightly, the corners of his mouth twitching as if he wanted to say something, but he didn't. He simply looked at Alexander with those big blue eyes for a long moment, then turned and walked away, the man holding his hand falling in step beside him.

Alexander watched them go and knew there was nothing he could do about it. All of the men he had been with over the centuries, seducing even the most reluctant conquest, he had never been rejected. He would, though, have traded all of those encounters to be the one walking towards the elevators with Noah. His Noah.

The numbness inside his chest suddenly gave away to a searing pain. He inhaled sharply and thought he saw Noah start to look over his shoulder. Suddenly, he didn't want to see the face that had been haunting his waking and sleeping thoughts. He wanted that face wiped out of his mind completely.

He spun around, his heart pounding against his ribs so loudly that he could barely hear anything else. He moved faster than he should have, barely managing to keep himself in check. Instead of taking the stairs or getting on another elevator to go back to his room, he headed back into the venue. He'd barely gone two feet inside before *he* was there, all tall and muscular, with those curls and dark eyes.

Alexander didn't even hesitate. He crossed the last of the space between them in two quick strides. Mason opened his mouth, as if to say something that would be possibly charming but more likely some awful cliché pick-up line, but the moment Alexander's hand closed around his, the jaw snapped shut and Mason followed.

Alexander had a feeling his father was staring disapprovingly after him, but he didn't turn to look. He didn't want to know. He didn't want to care about anything and drowning himself in Mason seemed like the best way to avoid having to think or feel. A night with someone who looked like they should be on the cover of one of those trashy romance books Shianne was always reading should do wonders to soothe the pain in his heart.

The hallway was empty except for the security guards Alexander barely even registered. He could hear one of the cameramen running after him, but ignored that as well. Screw what Gregory wanted. If the world was going to see Noah walking around with his new little 'friend' then they could see that Alexander wasn't sitting home and moping. No, he was still the playboy who could get any man he wanted...

Except the one he really wanted.

Alexander shook his head as he pulled Mason onto the elevator.

"I've been following your work from the moment it was announced," Mason said, his deep voice sounding loud against the canned music pumped into the elevator car. "Actually, I've been following your whole family since I was in college and I'd always wondered why you weren't one of the models. I mean, you're gorgeous enough."

Alexander pressed his lips together to keep himself from telling Mason to just shut up. He wasn't interested in someone stroking his ego. If he'd realized that the blogger was so talkative, he might've gone for someone else. The words began to fade away into a meaningless drone, but Mason didn't seem to notice that Alexander wasn't paying attention because he just kept talking.

The model Noah had been with was the second best-looking in the show, with Noah being the first, Alexander thought. Together, they were every straight woman's and gay man's fantasy. The other model had been tall and lean with dark hair and eyes. His face wasn't as pretty as Noah's, but it was still gorgeous. The press were going to have a field day when the two of them were finally caught together.

"This is your room?"

Mason's awe-struck question cut through Alexander's thoughts as he led the handsome man into his room. He gave Mason his most charming smile, the one that had never failed to get a man into his bed.

"It is," he answered. "And that's my bed."

Mason swallowed hard, his Adam's apple bobbing.

Alexander raised an eyebrow. "Well?" When Mason just stared at him, uncomprehendingly, Alexander sighed. "Am I really going to have to do everything?" His tone was teasing, coaxing a smile from the other man.

As Mason took off his jacket, the image of Noah and his model flashed into Alexander's mind again and he tried to push it away. It went, but was replaced by the memory of how distant Noah had been when they'd talked. Alexander scowled. He didn't want to think about the way Noah hadn't held his gaze, how stiff he'd been. He didn't want to think about anything; that's why Mason was there.

Alexander crossed to where Mason was working to unbutton his shirt and grabbed handfuls of the material and tugged. Buttons popped and fabric ripped. Moments later, shreds of what had been clothing were scattered around the floor and the vampire was rolling Mason underneath him. Both were down to just their underwear: Alexander in a black pair of his own design and Mason in, strangely enough, blue boxers with gold stars on them. Not that Alexander cared what Mason's underwear looked like. All he cared about was losing himself in the feel and taste of another person.

That's what Noah was doing.

The thought popped into Alexander's head, making his jaw clench. He didn't want to think about it, but the images rushed forward and he was unable to stop them.

The model kissing his way down Noah's body. Noah writhing beneath the touch of another. Two bodies entwined...

Alexander pulled back suddenly, leaving Mason leaning back on the bed, waiting. He didn't hear the other man asking if everything was all right. All he could hear was blood pumping, air rushing in and out of his lungs, his heart beating faster than it had in months. Alexander reached up and buried his fingers in Mason's soft curls. He pulled Mason's head to the side, using his other hand to hold the larger man's shoulder. He could almost taste the coppery liquid beneath the tanned skin. He leaned forward, opening his mouth...

"What the hell?!" Mason shoved against Alexander's chest hard enough to get the Vamp's attention. If Mason had been any smaller, it probably wouldn't have worked.

Alexander blinked and stared down in horror. What had he almost done? He let Mason shove him to one side and watched as the other man, shouting curses, grabbed the ruined clothes from the floor and stalked to the door. Alexander followed in a daze, barely getting one foot in front of the other. What had come over him? He hadn't lost control like that since the eighteen hundreds.

Mason was gone by the time Alexander reached the door to his suite. He glanced out into the hallway to see one of the cameramen staring at him with wide eyes. This one had to have been new because the others wouldn't have been phased by a half-naked man running from Alexander's room. He was professional enough, however, to have the camera rolling.

Alexander looked at the camera, forcing a lecherous smirk onto his face. "He couldn't handle it."

The door slammed shut and the Vamp sank to the floor and buried his head in his hands.

CHAPTER TEN

Erickson could feel Shianne's eyes on him as he paced. He knew she was worried. The two of them could always read the other's emotions, no matter how good of a mask they put up. Sometimes it was a good thing, but times like now, it wasn't. Erickson was the oldest, technically anyway, and he'd always felt that it was his job to protect the younger Vamps, particularly Shianne. He didn't always do a good job of it, he knew, and that was especially true lately, but his intentions were always good.

He almost laughed at that. Heir was always reminding his kids of the human saying about a road paved with good intentions. He ran his hand through his hair, a gesture he'd thought he'd gotten rid of decades ago. He'd always felt that it made him appear young and self-conscious.

"Dad will be here in, like, a half hour," Shianne reminded him unnecessarily.

He glared at her. "I know that, Shi."

She raised an eyebrow. "Any idea what you're going to say to him?"

He laughed a short bark of a laugh. "Are you kidding? All I've been doing for the past day and a half is trying to figure out what to tell Dad, and I still have no idea."

"Have you thought about maybe the truth?" Shianne crossed her arms, then winced.

Erickson turned towards her. "Okay, I have to say it. I don't get why you had to get a boob job. You never have any problem getting guys' attention. Was it just to make Val happy?"

Shianne sat up straight in her chair. "Excuse me? You, of all people, are going to question cosmetic surgery?"

"What's that supposed to mean?"

She rolled her eyes. "Your teeth, idiot. Was there really a point in getting them capped with titanium or did you just feel the need to set off metal detectors for the rest of your life?"

He bared his fangs at her, then dropped down into the closest chair with a sigh.

"Did picking a fight with me make you feel any better?" Shianne asked as she crossed one tanned leg over the other.

"You knew that's what I was doing?" Erickson asked.

"Of course," Shianne said. "I know you, Erickson. Being an ass-hat is your go-to when you're upset."

A part of him wanted to come up with an insult in return to get her going, but she was right. He wasn't really annoyed with her and it hadn't made him forget what was really upsetting him. He spread his hands wide and gave his sister a pleading look.

"What am I supposed to do?"

Shianne's face was serious and almost sad, an expression she never would've had if the cameras had been around. She leaned forward and put her hand on Erickson's knee. "I'm sorry, big brother. I don't know."

****

"I am surprised that you did not wish to go to the airport to meet your father and brother," Rupa said as she and Pru slowly walked through the gardens.

Pru chewed at her nail, waiting for the scolding that Di usually gave. It didn't come. Instead, she looked up to see her grandmother looking down at her with an expression of concern. It wasn't like when Val or Shianne gave her that look. No matter how much they wanted to help her, she always had the feeling that they were more worried that they wouldn't be able to handle whatever it was that was bothering her. She didn't blame them. Shianne wasn't her mom, and even though Val was technically her stepmother and tried the best she could, it was just different.

"Is there something bothering you, Prussia?" Rupa asked, her hazel eyes searching her grand-daughter's face.

Pru nodded. "That's why I didn't want to go," she admitted. "I wanted a chance to talk to you before Dad got here." She glanced over her shoulder at the cameraman trailing along behind and scowled. She'd been hoping he'd follow Erickson and Shianne, but they'd disappeared, off to talk somewhere or something. They'd been doing that a lot lately, she thought. Perhaps it had something to do with why Erickson had been acting so weird lately. She mentally shook herself. She had something else on her mind right now. She could worry about her oldest brother after her talk with Rupa.

"Have a seat." Rupa gestured to an elegantly carved stone bench that sat beneath a pair of twined olive trees.

Pru sat down and scrubbed her palms against her shorts. They weren't sweating, but she just felt like she needed to do something with her hands. She never knew what to do with her hands.

"It seems you have had something on your mind since you first arrived," Rupa said. "Though I suspect you have been mulling over this for much longer."

Pru nodded. She'd talked to Val about it, but she needed to talk to someone who would be able to understand. Val was Turned. It was different for her.

"Leo turned sixteen," she blurted out.

Rupa nodded. "So your father told me."

"But I'm still twelve," Pru continued. Her chest was tight. It was harder to get the words out than she'd thought it would be. "And I don't know when that will change. Or if it will." She looked up at her grandmother and felt her eyes burning with tears. She forced them back, refusing to cry.

"You are worried about Settling as you are," Rupa said softly.

Pru nodded, swallowing hard around the lump in her throat. "I don't want to be twelve forever. I don't even want to be thirteen or fourteen forever."

"You want to grow up." There was understanding in Rupa's voice that couldn't exist in Val's because Val didn't understand what it was like to age slowly and fear it stopping too early.

Pru nodded again. "I tried talking to Val about it..." her voice trailed off. She didn't want to say anything about her stepmother that sounded bad.

"Valencia was Turned." Rupa gave voice to Pru's thoughts. "She was not Born and so cannot understand what it is like to experience the world passing by so fast as one creeps along, always wondering at what point you will stop. First, it is the fear of being too young, then it becomes anxiety as you reach the age at which you would wish to Settle. Finally, you see the hints of gray, the lines on the skin, and pray that no more will come before that time."

"Exactly!" Pru nodded. She'd known her grandmother would understand.

"Have you talked to your father or your brothers or sisters?"

She shook her head, scowling. "Everyone's so busy with their tan sprays, underwear models and the television show to have any time to talk to me." She crossed her arms and knew she looked every bit the bratty tween. "Then there was the whole thing with Taylor Ann." She suddenly realized how that sounded and hurried to clarify. "I'm glad she's doing better and she really did need all of us supporting her."

"I know you love your sister." Rupa reached over and put her hand over Pru's. "And it is quite normal to wish for the attention of those you love."

"I don't want attention." Pru fought to keep from yelling. She wasn't angry with her grandmother, just with everything else. "I just want someone to listen to me."

"I am listening."

The calm way Rupa said the words helped push back Pru's anger. She was right. She was listening. Pru continued, "I don't know what to do. It's too much for me to handle. Sometimes I feel like everything is just going to explode out of me and there's nothing I can do to stop it."

"I have lived for a very long time, Prussia. Years that make your hundred and eighty-seven seem nothing more than a blink of the eye," Rupa spoke slowly.

Pru listened, soothed by her grandmother's voice as much as her words.

"Long before you were born, even before your father was born, I decided how I wanted to live my life, and I believe that is what has kept me content these long centuries." Rupa paused, glancing down as if to check if Pru was listening. "I choose not to see the world in an Age of Coming or an Age of Going, but rather in an Age of Present."

Pru frowned. That sounded nice, but she had no clue what it meant. Fortunately, Rupa offered an explanation.

"Many of our kind are consumed with the past, obsessed over

things that have been finished for centuries. Others fear the future. They have seen wars and plagues, advancements of technology that have given us both good and evil. They know that nothing is certain and this uncertainty preoccupies their minds."

With a start, Pru realized that was her and Leo. She was terrified of what the future would hold, but Leo was obsessed with the past, with finding answers to questions that Pru was beginning to suspect weren't limited to their vampiric origins.

"So what do you do?" Pru asked.

"Live in the present. Do not worry about what tomorrow may hold, but rather enjoy the moment you are experiencing right now." She looked up at the trees above them. "These trees have lived here for nearly a millennium. Should we think back over the years and pick out the ones where no fruit was borne, trying to decided why it happened? Or should we worry that this year, they will bear no fruit? Rather, I believe we should enjoy the beauty of the branches and leaves, appreciate the strength in the trunks, all things we have now, in the moment. It does not mean that bad will not come, but that it will not remain with us forever, nor mar the time we are experiencing at this very moment, whether by haunting us from the past or taunting us from the future."

Silence fell for several minutes as Pru thought over what her grandmother had said. She half expected Rupa to break the quiet, to ask if there was anything else, then excuse herself because she had other things to do. She didn't though. Instead, Rupa stayed where she was, her eyes slowly roaming around the garden, as if enjoying the time to simply sit and observe nature.

Her grandmother wasn't just saying all of those things, Pru realized. She truly believed it. Maybe, Pru thought, that was why Rupa always seemed to have this whole aura of peace around her. She was never worried or thinking about the past. It was all about the now.

Pru took a slow, deep breath, then let it out. Maybe this whole 'in the moment' thing was something she should check out. It didn't sound like it was easy, but if it could get rid of the anxiety that was always gnawing at her insides, it would be worth the hard work.

"Thank you," she said. She stood and looked down at her grandmother, a thought occurring to her. "Maybe you should talk to Leo about your life philosophy." She chose her words carefully, not wanting to sound like she was tattling on her older brother to their grandmother and the rest of the world. "He's a bit...preoccupied with vampire history."

Rupa nodded, her face sad. "Your brother believes that he cannot move forward until he has answered questions about his past."

Pru was surprised. That sounded a lot like what the fortune-teller from a couple months ago had told her. In fact, now that she thought about it, Madame Tauna had read her cards and given her similar advice to what her grandmother had just said. It wasn't about choosing when to Settle, but how she was going to live her life until then.

"You have thought of something," Rupa observed.

"Did you know that the network hired a fortune teller a couple months ago?" Pru asked.

"Your father told me," Rupa said. Her eyes widened in understanding. "She read you and your brother."

Pru nodded. When she spoke again, she lowered her voice, angling herself so that her back was to the camera. "Can Tarot card readings be real? I mean, she had to be a fake, right?"

Rupa shook her head slowly, a thoughtful expression on her face. "The power of the second sight has dimmed over the centuries, but I remember when it was once strong amongst my people, the ones who would come to be known as gypsies. It is quite possible that she is from one of the few bloodlines who still possess it."

Pru stared at her grandmother. Sure, Madam Tauna had freaked her out with the stuff she'd known, but once she'd gotten away, out of the shadows and into the modern world she knew, the possibility of a true reading had faded from her mind. She'd convinced herself that it had to be fake, and now her grandmother was saying that it might have been real.

"It bothers you," Rupa said suddenly. "That this woman could truly have had the Sight."

Pru nodded. "She read me and Leo both."

"Does it worry you more what she said to him than what she said to you?"

"What she said to Leo," Pru whispered. The words echoed in her mind. She hadn't been able to forget them.

You lost the lady at an early age and are afraid you will forget. The hooded man took her from you, burnt her flesh, spoke the words over her body, brought death into your house. Secrets and lies protect him, prevent you from your mission. The absence of this knowledge has driven you your whole life. You asked for the past, but there is future in here as well. This point in your history shaped everything you are, everything you do and will continue to do so. And when the time comes, when the truth is revealed in its entirety, you will be the one to sit in judgement, to decide fates. There is darkness and light both in you, Leo Vamp, and your choice at that time will decide which will triumph.

She shivered. No one else had heard the reading, just her, Leo and her best friends Sunny and Karson. She'd sworn them both to secrecy, unsure why she didn't want anyone else to know what had been said. When the network had called Heir to say that something had gone wrong with the cameras and only Karson's reading had been recorded, she hadn't been able to stop the twist in her stomach. Even then, she realized, she'd known the truth of what Madame Tauna was, she just hadn't wanted to admit it to herself.

Rupa's hands wrapping around hers startled her back to the present. Her grandmother's face was earnest. "Do not speak of what she read until you feel that it is absolutely necessary. Only then must you disclose and only to the person you feel led to choose."

Pru nodded. Suddenly, she didn't want to be here anymore. She wanted to be at home, safe in her bedroom, laying on her bed and trolling online blogs for the latest news on Alexander and Noah. That was safe. This, whatever this was, she had a bad feeling was the furthest thing from safe she'd ever known.

CHAPTER ELEVEN

Darius Murdoch moved them through the paparazzi with ease – most of the reporters were considerably smaller than the former college football star and cop – but he couldn't stop the barrage of thickly accented questions being shouted their way, most of which were directed at Alexander.

Someone, it seemed, had spotted he and Noah leaving with their respective...whatevers.

"Alexander, did you know that Noah was cheating on you?"

"Were you cheating on him first?"

"How long have the two of you been broken up?"

"Was this whole relationship a publicity stunt?"

Alexander flinched at that one, but didn't say a word. He hadn't actually said much of anything since his father had shown up at his door the next morning with a plain-looking woman who Alexander thought he should have recognized. He hadn't even considered asking her name, and if his father hadn't been there, he would have just sent her on her way. As it was, he'd only taken a swallow, enough to ensure his father would be satisfied. They'd then ridden to the airport in silence and maintained almost the same level of quiet for the entire flight.

"I didn't realize the reporters would be worse here than at home," Di spoke from where she stood next to the limo they would be taking to Rupa's. She glared at the people airport security were now herding backwards.

Alexander climbed into the car, dreading the hundreds of questions his siblings would pepper him with. Erickson about the business end. Shianne about the celebrities. Pru about...Alexander frowned. He didn't want to think about Noah.

"Hey, Alexander."

He settled in his seat and looked up to see that only Taylor Ann was sitting across from him. Well, her and a handsome man in his late twenties. Tall, lean with blond hair and warm brown eyes. It was a testament to how numb Alexander was that he didn't feel the slightest bit of attraction to Taylor Ann's therapist.

"Taylor Ann," he forced a partial smile. "Stephen." He found it odd that the therapist didn't want to be called doctor, but it wasn't really his business.

Taylor Ann frowned as Di and Heir climbed into the limo, Di taking the seat next to Stephen so she could sit across from Heir and discuss whatever it was she and Heir talked about. Taylor Ann leaned forward and put her hand on Alexander's knee. She pitched her voice low enough that the words would be lost in the other conversation.

"Are you okay?"

Alexander nodded, but he could see that she didn't believe him. She didn't push it though, not like Shianne or Pru or even Erickson would've. The only other Vamp would would've sat back without asking again would've been Leo, but he wouldn't have asked anything in the first place. Leo didn't really register things on the same level as everyone else.

"I'm here," Taylor Ann added, then turned the conversation elsewhere. "Pru wanted to stay with Grandmother. Leo, of course, is holed up the library."

Alexander could've sworn that his father tensed at that statement, but Heir's face betrayed nothing as he continued his conversation with Di.

"It was weird though," Taylor Ann continued. "Erickson and Shianne disappeared just before we were getting ready to leave. I don't think I've ever seen either one of them pass up the chance to..." Taylor Ann paused, took a deep breath, and appeared to choose a different ending to the sentence. "Interact with the media."

She was right, but Alexander couldn't muster up enough emotion to care. Besides, it wasn't the two older Vamps who the paparazzi wanted to torment at the moment. The rumors about Erickson and that singer were old news now. He and Noah's relationship...a sharp pain went through him. He was just grateful they weren't back home. Everything there would be a reminder of *him*. Maybe in Greece Alexander could find a distraction.

He hoped so, he thought as he looked out the window, not registering any of the beautiful scenery going by as they headed for the staircase that would lead them to his grandmother's house. If he couldn't find someone or something to get his mind off of *him*, Alexander wasn't sure how long he'd be able to keep up the charade.

****

It was late by the time Erickson was able to work up the courage to tell Heir and Di that he needed to speak with them. He'd asked Shianne and she'd agreed that it would be better to tell the two of them together than to only tell Heir. Di was going to be pissed when she found out that they'd hidden this from her, but if Heir was there, her visible reaction would probably less intense. Shianne, of course, came with him. Neither of them had talked about, but they really hadn't needed to. He definitely didn't want to do this on his own.

They went to Heir's room as it was the largest guest room in the house. He immediately sat down in the chair by the window and Di took the chair to his right. After a quick exchange of looks, Erickson and Shianne both sat on the love-seat opposite their father.

Silence.

"You wished to tell us something?" Heir prompted.

Erickson looked at Shianne who gave him a 'go-head' gesture.

He resisted the urge to tell her that didn't help. As much as he hated it, she was right. He'd gotten himself into this mess. He had to own up to it and see what it was his father needed to do to fix it.

"So, uh, you know those tabloid stories that've been going around for the past few weeks?" He rubbed his hands together. "The ones about me and, uh, Tedi, the singer?"

Di pursed her lips and nodded. Heir inclined his head ever so slightly.

"Well, her attorney called and said that the rumors are true. At least, the her being pregnant part."

"Her attorney called?" Heir asked mildly. He raised an eyebrow.

Erickson knew this was one of those times where a human's face would be turning red. "Um, yes. I mean, not me, but he called Ibrahim and then Ibrahim called me."

"Ibrahim called you and not Heir or myself?" Di asked.

"He called the house," Erickson explained. "I just happened to answer the phone. He said your cell kept sending him to voicemail and this wasn't the kind of thing he wanted to just leave a message about."

"Is the attorney requesting a paternity test?" Heir asked.

Erickson gave his father a surprised look. Heir was highly intelligent, but with so many centuries of ever-changing technology, it was hard to keep up, even for him.

"Tedi's saying she hasn't been with anyone else in four months," Shianne supplied.

"Still," Di said. "Paternity must be determined before any other decisions can be made."

Decisions? Erickson blinked. What was there to decide?

"If not for a DNA test, then why did her lawyer call ours?" Heir asked.

"Oh, um," Erickson stumbled around for the answer, pulling his thoughts away from future decisions.

Shianne answered this one as well. "She's claiming Erickson drugged her."

Di's eyes narrowed and even Heir looked at his son sharply. It was Di who asked the question though. "Did you?"

"No!" Erickson was appalled. "How could you think I'd do something like that?"

"I didn't mean intentionally," Di quickly clarified. "I don't believe you would hurt anyone intentionally like that. I wasn't sure if you'd been using anything recreationally."

He shook his head. "I brought wine. That was it." He waited to see if Shianne was going to add the part about his persuasiveness, but she remained silent.

"Did you feed on her?" Di's look was so severe that Erickson wanted to lie, but he knew it would be better to get it all out now. Besides, if he copped to this, maybe they wouldn't ask about persuasion.

"Yes," he muttered. He hadn't said he'd be proud with the admission.

Di cursed in her native language. Erickson had heard it before, but had never asked what it meant. He was pretty sure it wasn't good.

"Here is what we will do," Heir said, his voice calm. "First, we must discover if the child is indeed Erickson's. A Settled Vampire reproducing with a human is rare to say the least."

"And if it is mine?" Erickson reached for his sister's hand.

"Then you will take responsibility for your actions," Heir said sternly. "As I would expect any child of mine to do."

Erickson was afraid to ask what that would mean, sure he wouldn't like it. As Heir began to explain exactly what this responsibility would entail, Erickson knew he'd been right. He didn't like it at all. He squeezed Shianne's hand and hoped that the test would prove that he wasn't the father of Tedi's baby. If he was, everything was going to change.

CHAPTER TWELVE

Leo paused outside Di's room on his way back to the guest room where he was currently residing. Normally, he would have been too preoccupied with his research to have even noticed the hushed voices coming from behind the door, but tonight he was attempting to be more aware of his surroundings. He did not want to be caught by his father while exploring his grandmother's house. He had not yet found anything of use, but there remained so much more to explore. If Heir discovered that Leo was investigating here in a place that might very well hold the answers to everything, Leo was certain he would not be without someone at his side for the remainder of their time in Greece. They would be leaving for Paris in sixteen days.

The reasons for his stopping did not matter as he registered the discussion his father was having with his brother. He assumed Di and Shianne were also in the room, but they were not speaking. The only one who was talking was Heir. And he was telling

Erickson that if the girl was pregnant, steps would be taken to ensure responsibility was taken.

Leo's eyes widened. He had never understood his siblings' fascinations with humans and considered mating with them to be beneath a true vampire, though he had never said these things to anyone in his family. He had understood that his view would be insulting to the others. Besides, he admitted, he had no right to advise on romantic relationships when he himself had never had one. In truth, never desired one. He did not deem it fair to lecture others on who they should love when he had never been in love.

He heard movement from inside the room and hurried away, slipping inside his room just as the door to his father's room opened. He carefully closed the door and leaned back against it, his mind racing. For once, his thoughts were not of the past, but rather of the future. If he had heard correctly, everything for the Vamp family was going to change when they returned to America, and he did not know how he felt about a half-human, half-vampire being a part of the mix.

A thought suddenly hit him. Something good would come of this, he realized. If Heir and Di would be dealing with this situation, they would not notice what he was doing. Erickson's dalliance with a human may very well prove to give Leo the time he needed to find his answers.

****

It had taken Shianne nearly an hour to fall asleep the night before and she knew it showed. She'd seen the dark circles under her eyes when she'd woken up and had applied so much make-up that even she thought it was almost too much. Finding the perfect shade to match her Vamp Tramp spray was difficult and applying it took a lot of skill. By the time she was satisfied with her appearance, it was almost mid-morning.

She hurried down the stairs, looking for the rest of her family. She frowned as she passed by empty room after empty room. Where had everyone gone?

"Is you looking for family?"

Shianne put on her most charming smile as she turned to face Aris. The intelligence in his eyes said that his broken English had nothing to do with how smart he was. She liked that. Usually she preferred her men pretty and stupid – basically, the male versions of the women Erickson slept with – but she thought it might be nice to not just have a nice face to look at but someone who could actually hold a conversation, even if it was in his broken English and her bad Greek.

"Yes," she said. "Have you seen them?"

Aris nodded. "Rupa ta-takes them to see market."

"Why didn't you go with them?" Not that she was complaining. She leaned against the wall, trying to be casual while showing off all of her best assets.

He shrugged. "I have seen market." He looked at her then, his dark eyes warm, but puzzled. "Is this Amer-American fashion?" His tongue tied over the words as he pointed at the arm she had leaning on the wall.

"Is what an American fashion?" Shianne asked.

"To match house color with skin."

Shianne looked down, her mouth falling open when she saw what he meant. Her tanning spray was on so thick that her skin was the same orangish color as her grandmother's walls. If she'd been human, her face would've been bright red. She swore and tried to hurry away, completely mortified. A hand around her arm stopped her. She looked up and found Aris looking down at her, his expression one of concern now.

"I upset you?" He shook his head, concern turning into something else. "No, I-I not..."

He ran his hand through his hair as he let loose a stream of Greek curses that Shianne didn't need to know the meaning of to catch the gist.

Aris's reaction was enough to push back her embarrassment. He hadn't been making fun of her. His question, as strange as it had seemed, had been an honest one. Then again, she thought, perhaps it wasn't so weird after all. He did spend all of his time up here with Rupa, and from what Shianne observed, this wasn't exactly the most pop culture friendly house in the world. She wondered if Aris had ever seen her show.

"It's okay." She reached out and grabbed his arm. Her eyebrows shot up. Damn, he was firm. "Aris," she said his name. "It's okay."

He looked at her, his expression strangely anxious. "O-kay?"

"I'm not upset anymore." She wrapped her arms around his and peered up at him. "But since everyone else has gone, it looks like you're going to have to entertain me." She wasn't sure how much of what she'd said he'd understood until he looked down at her with a soft smile on his face and nodded.

Suddenly, she was glad the others hadn't waited for her. She had a feeling she and Aris were going to get along just fine.

*****

Taylor Ann could feel the eyes on her as she walked through the market. She knew that it wasn't just her people were looking at, but rather the whole family. It didn't make her any less self-conscious. What did help with that was the man walking next to her, his very presence helping her to stay calm.

She would've thought, if anyone had asked her, that someone with body issues like hers would never be able to trust an attractive member of the opposite sex. Or, she supposed, the same sex, if that was their thing. Then again, she'd always felt like women were trying to find fault in her appearance, though they were generally meaner about it. She wasn't sure if a woman therapist would've been a better first thought. Not that she would've traded Stephen for anyone, male or female. She shivered, thinking about what her life would be like if he hadn't been the one hired to help her.

"You're doing it again." Stephen leaned across her to pick up something from a street booth, pitching his voice low, for her ears only.

His quiet voice did what it had been doing for the past two

months and brought her out of her head. That was part of her problem, they'd discovered. She spent far too much time in her own head.

Taylor smiled at him, a true genuine smile. She gestured to his hand. "Nice scarf."

Stephen grinned as he held up the scrap of green silk. "Not my style?"

Taylor laughed. One of the things she loved about how Stephen treated her was his subtly. He always made sure the humans couldn't hear him when he had to talk to her about something private, and tried to keep the Vamps from hearing as much as possible. He understood how much she cared about what her family thought of her.

As she thought about them, she glanced around, her good mood fading. No one had realized that Shianne wasn't with them until they'd gone over a mile. Erickson hadn't said a word when Heir had said that if Shianne wanted to catch up with them, it was up to her. In fact, Erickson hadn't said much all day. His face looked paler than usual and he wasn't flirting with any of the dozen or so women who'd been eyeing him for the past twenty minutes.

Taylor Ann frowned. Then there was Alexander. She knew why he was moping around, even if no one else in the family had been paying attention. Well, she amended, no one but Pru. Over the past two months, she'd come realize just how much attention the littlest Vamp paid to all the rest of them. With Alexander though, it seemed like the only thing people were talking about was his fabulous clothing line. She doubted a single one of the others – aside from Pru – knew that things had fallen apart between Alexander and his human.

Leo seemed normal enough, she supposed. It was so hard to tell with him. Her youngest brother was still such a mystery to her. He actually wasn't scowling, which she supposed was a first. He hadn't complained at all when Heir had insisted they all go down through the market. Now she suspected that Leo's compliance had more to do with the carvings on some of the ancient architecture than a desire to spend time with the family.

Taylor Ann's eyes went to Val and Pru who were walking on either side of Rupa. Pru actually seemed happier than she had been in a while. Taylor Ann smiled softly. Even when Pru was being a pain the butt, she couldn't really be mad at her little sister. It was those eyes. Treasa's eyes. Out of the four younger children, Taylor Ann remembered their mother the best. Sometimes, Taylor Ann wondered how things would've turned out differently if Treasa hadn't died.

"Taylor." Stephen's hand on her wrist drew her back this time. His eyes were full of concern. "What's wrong?"

Taylor Ann sighed. "I was just thinking about how it doesn't seem fair that when I'm finally feeling better than I have in years, my family seems to be having issues." It still felt a bit strange to be this open with someone, to say what she was thinking, but she also felt relief that she didn't have to hold it inside anymore.

"You are not responsible for your family's happiness," Stephen said sternly. "We've talked about this."

Taylor Ann nodded. "You're right, but I just don't like seeing them unhappy."

Stephen's expression softened and he squeezed her wrist. "I know, but they have to figure things out for themselves too. All you can do is be there for them when they need you."

He was right, she knew, but it still sucked.

CHAPTER THIRTEEN

Erickson wasn't entirely sure if he was supposed to greet Tedi, compliment her or ignore her. He was great when he was supposed to be charming people and he wasn't bad at being a jerk when it came to legal stuff, but this was completely new ground for him. Especially considering he was looking at Tedi and her three lawyers over Skype. He could also see Ibrahim off to one side, as if the lawyer was trying to be visible but also still be seen as sitting next to his clients.

Erickson glanced towards the door again, waiting for his sister to defy their father's instructions and join him. She didn't though. Heir had been quite insistent that it be only the three of them. Father, son and Di. Outside of the three of them, only Shianne knew what this meeting was about, so Heir hadn't included Val. Why he'd forbidden Shianne from coming, Erickson didn't know, but he didn't like it. What if the lawyers asked for his side of the story? Shouldn't his sister be here to back him up? She knew what had really happened...

Oh. The realization hit him. Shianne knew what had really happened. Heir believed that Erickson hadn't drugged Tedi, but now Erickson knew that his father at least suspected the use of a little extra persuasion. While neither Erickson nor Alexander were strong enough to force someone into doing something they didn't really want to do, they did lower inhibitions enough that they could coax people into giving in to what they really wanted. Tedi had been attracted to him, but she'd also thought he was a jerk. He'd just...willed her to forget that part.

The thing was, humans didn't know about any of the Vamps little gifts. Like Erickson, Alexander was very persuasive. Pru's agility and almost feline gracefulness was beyond what other vampires had. Di didn't need to compel as she had the ability to soothe anxiety and suggest that certain memories be forgotten. That particular ability had been quite useful when they'd been hiding their feedings. Now, she was much pickier about when she used it.

And it wasn't just about revealing their secrets, Erickson knew. If it got out what any of them could do, things were going to go from reality shows and the fashion industry to cages and stakes. Vampires were immortal, not eternal. They could be killed; it just took more to do it. People being pissed off because they thought their celebrities manipulated them was definitely one way to do it.

A touch on his hand made Erickson straighten in his seat. The meeting was beginning. Heir had told Erickson to be quiet and not answer any questions unless Ibrahim cleared it, so he sat with his hands folded in his lap and listened.

"As I see that you have all joined us for this meeting rather than sending a single representative, it means you have the paternity test results," Heir said, not bothering with any pleasantries.

"We do," the lawyer in the middle said. Apparently he was the one in charge. He slid a folder across the table to Ibrahim. "Mr. Demir said that you had a proposal for us?"

Heir didn't answer, but rather spoke to his attorney. "Ibrahim?"

"It's the real thing," Ibrahim said. His eyes flicked over to Erickson who looked away. "The tests confirm that Erickson is the father."

Erickson heard a rushing sound in his ears almost as if he'd held up two of those seashells that could let you 'hear the ocean.' He suddenly felt dizzy and light-headed, something that had never happened to him before. He hadn't realized it until the moment the words had come out of Ibrahim's mouth that he'd still been thinking this entire thing was going to blow over. He'd spend a couple months in the dog house with his father, but it would go away eventually and everything would get back to normal. Now, he knew nothing would.

Dimly, he was aware of his father speaking, but he only knew what Heir was saying because they'd talked about it two nights ago. He heard the words but they were almost meaningless.

"We will fully pay all medical expenses, of course," Heir said. "And we will also pay for Miss Mitchell to go on an extended vacation before the rumors can no longer be denied."

Erickson almost asked who Miss Mitchell was, then he realized that must've been Tedi's last name. He'd never known it. That seemed like something he should have known.

"We will include compensation for her missed touring time as well," Heir continued. "But we will expect a non-disclosure agreement to be signed as we will be using our resources to discredit this story. Should Miss Mitchell want to keep the child, we will provide a backstory." He paused for a moment, and then went on. "But should she decide that she does not want the child, we will ask that full custody be signed over to Erickson along with the NDA."

"I don't want it," Tedi spoke for the first time. "I don't like kids and I never wanted them." Her face was tight. "I only stayed pregnant because they told me to, just for now." She jerked her head towards the attorneys.

Erickson felt his hands curl into fists. She had planned on getting rid of the baby? His baby? A flare of anger went through him and it helped clear his head and focus him. Sure, he was absolutely terrified of being a father and he'd spent quite a bit of the last couple months wishing he'd never agreed to be in that stupid music video, but he'd never considered...his mouth flattened. No. There was only one thing more important to him than his own wants, and that was family. No matter how it happened, how unexpected it was, or what it was going to do to his life, that baby was family.

"Then we'll have the paperwork drawn up and faxed over." The words came out of his mouth before he'd realized he was going to say them. Heir and Di both gave him startled looks, but he didn't look away from Tedi. She looked as shocked as he suspected everyone else was. "I don't walk away from my responsibilities." He resisted the urge to look at his father. "Or from my family."

****

Taylor Ann could feel tears burning in her eyes and she struggled not to cry. Now that she was getting healthier, her body was able to produce tears, but that didn't mean she wanted them. She stared down at the laptop screen, as if she could will them to go away.

"Should I have not told you?" Pru looked worried.

"No," Taylor Ann said faintly. "I'm glad you did. It would've been worse if we'd gotten hit with questions unprepared."

She heard Pru leave the room, but she couldn't tear her eyes away from the online tabloid magazine. Someone had taken pictures of her and Stephen. The gestures were innocent, but when strung together with a headline that read "Sexy Therapist Boinking Vamp Patient," they looked like something else entirely.

This was awful. Her chest began to tighten. Everything Stephen had done to help her and this was how she repaid him? These horrible people that snuck pictures and made them out to be something they weren't were going to ruin his reputation.

"Taylor Ann?" Stephen's voice came from the doorway. "Pru

said you needed me."

She pointed at the computer without a word. He came over and sat down next to her. She closed her eyes and waited for him to tell her that he hated her, that he was through with her, that she wasn't worth him losing his career.

What she didn't expect was to hear him laugh.

Her eyes opened and she finally turned away from the screen. He was chuckling until he looked at her and then the sound faded as he seemed to realize that she wasn't finding this funny.

"They're saying..." She couldn't even bring herself to say it. "This will ruin you."

Stephen's face was serious now. "It's a tabloid, Taylor. And there's no truth to it."

"But people don't care if it's the truth," she said. She had to make him understand. "They love scandal. They like to see people fail and get hurt. It doesn't matter that it's not true, or that you'd never sleep with any patient, much less me. They'll talk like it's true and your reputation will be ruined."

He put his hand over hers, giving it a light squeeze before returning it to his lap. "I'm not going to stop helping you simply because some ass-hats are trying to make money with lies."

"What if–"

"Taylor."

Her name stopped whatever else she was going to say. He was the only one who called her that. Just Taylor. Not Taylor Ann.

"Let me deal with this." He closed the laptop. "This is my

responsibility, not yours. And no arguing about it."

A ghost of a smile curved her lips. "All right," she said. "We'll just have to make sure there's space between us from here on out. Make sure no one else gets pictures–"

"Taylor, stop." His voice was firm. "We are not changing the way we do things." He hesitated and clarified, "Unless it bothers you."

She shook her head. They'd discussed how her pushing people away emotionally had resulted in a lack of physical contact. He'd realized that she'd been craving that almost as much as she'd been craving the blood. She'd needed reassurances, but hadn't let anyone close enough to give them. Platonic touching helped ground her, helped her deal with things.

"Then we keep going and we don't worry about what anyone else says, just like I've been telling you these past couple months." He stood and looked down at her. "What kind of therapist would I be if I didn't take my own advice?"

Taylor Ann wasn't so sure she agreed with him, but she didn't argue as he walked out of the room with Pru's computer. She didn't know if this would blow over or not, but she was going to try her best to do what he'd said and let it go. It wasn't easy, but if these past two months had proven anything to her, it was that she was much stronger than she'd ever thought she'd be.

CHAPTER FOURTEEN

Leo knew he was taking a risk prowling around Rupa's library late at night, but he had run out of time. The family would be leaving tomorrow morning for Paris and he had yet to find anything in his grandmother's collection that could help him. The problem he now faced was that he had looked at the spine of every book, taken out the ones Heir did not have and read them, trying to find any hint at the secrets his father was keeping. He had seen nothing of the mark, or of the strange language on his papers.

He blew out a puff of air and brushed his hair back out of his eyes. He was vaguely aware that he had left dust across his forehead, but he did not care enough to try to wipe it away. His grandmother kept the library clean, but dust always found its way to books. He found it comforting that this seemed to be true no matter the book, nor its location.

"A sign," he said quietly. Whether he spoke to himself or to some unseen other, he did not know. "A sign to know that this is not a fool's errand. Not the quest of a son who cannot accept the truth." He closed his eyes and felt the heat of tears against his eyelids.

He had not cried since he was a child, not because he believed men or vampires should not cry, but rather because after the death of his mother, he had nothing left in his life to cry about. If something happened to another member of his family, he knew he would shed tears, but the mundane affairs of humans or of the heart did not touch him.

He rubbed his hands across his eyes. In all his decades of searching, he had never been this frustrated. He felt as if something was here, close enough for him to touch, but yet just outside his reach. It was as if something existed just beyond his peripheral vision. He could feel it and almost see it, but not focus on it.

He swore quietly and opened his eyes. He would not give up. If need be, he would stay in the library up until the moment of departure. He took a step forward and his elbow bumped against one of his grandmother's ancient statues. He had experienced difficulty adjusting to his growth since turning sixteen, but he was still fast and graceful enough to catch the sculpture before it fell.

As he steadied it, his fingers brushed against something of a different texture. Curious, he looked down, expecting to see an imperfection or chip at the base of the marble sculpture. Instead, what he saw took all of the air from his lungs. His heart thumped hard against his chest, harder than he had ever felt before. There it was. After two and a half weeks of searching, he had finally found the mark.

He picked up the statue, his hands running over the cool marble in search of another mark, anything that could tell him who may have carved the piece, or who would have placed this symbol upon it. Only after he had passed over it a third time did he admit that no further information could be obtained from the sculpture itself. But, he did not allow himself to become discouraged. He had a new lead. He would research the statue and discover its importance. The fact that he had not seen this symbol upon numerous objects lent to his theory that it was special. If it was special, then whatever it was put upon was also special.

A surge of energy went through him. He would begin here, but at least he knew now his search would not end in Greece. What better place to find information on art than in Paris? He moved towards the books again, this time in search of art and architecture.

****

"You know, Aris," Shianne said as she slowly walked alongside the human. "I think you've been the best teacher I've ever had."

He smiled down at her, his teeth flashing white against his bronzed skin. "You speak Greek much better now."

"And your English has improved also." Shianne chose her words carefully. It amused her that her broken Greek sounded to him like his English sounded to her.

"Thanks to you." Aris stopped in front of the marble fountain in the center of Rupa's garden.

The pair stood in silence, watching the moonlight ripple on the water. They had spent most of the past two weeks together. Erickson had been moping around so much that Shianne hadn't been able to stand being near him. She'd heard that he'd spoken out against Tedi not wanting the baby and that he'd agreed to take responsibility, and she'd been proud of him for that, but now he seemed to be in mourning for his carefree single life. She loved her brother, but she didn't have much sympathy for him at the moment. That's what happened when you weren't careful sleeping around. At least, she thought, she didn't have to worry about that. Settled female vampires couldn't get pregnant. It wasn't possible. She frowned as an inexplicable wave of sadness went over her.

"Are you sad?" Aris lightly touched her arm, the warmth of his human skin hot against hers.

Shianne could hear the worry in his voice but didn't look at him. She couldn't bear the thought of those dark eyes full of concern for her.

She shook her head. "It's nothing."

"Shi." He'd taken to the shortening of her name much easier than her full one. "I do not wish for you to be sad."

The Greek words made her shiver. She could still understand more than she could speak.

"You are cold?" Now he just sounded confused.

"No." One side of her mouth tipped up. She hadn't thought it was possible for him to be cuter, but whenever she happened to throw him off, he'd get this look that made her think of what he must've looked like when he was younger, still in his gawky teenage phase.

"Please explain."

She could hear the frustration in his voice and turned towards him. It must be difficult, she realized for the first time, to be a human in the vampire world. They could share all of the secrets, but there would always be a part of being a vampire that no human could ever understand. It was this thought that made her want to explain her behavior. Or at least part of it. She wasn't about to tell him that she'd shivered because she liked the sound of his voice, particularly when he spoke in his native tongue.

"I was just thinking about children," she said. "And how I can't have any. I'd never thought about it before and it made me a little sad."

Aris reached out and tucked a strand of her hair behind her ear. His fingers brushed over her cheek and Shianne felt another rush of warmth go through her, this one deeper than the one before. It had been a while since anyone had touched her like that. The Vamps weren't a very touchy family to begin with, and add that to the fact that any lover she took was human, which meant she didn't get attached, and sometimes she forgot what it was like. Very few men she'd been with in her centuries of life had taken the time to make the gentle gestures, and she'd never expected them to.

A sudden memory flashed through her mind. Her father and her step-mother. Not Val, but Treasa. They were standing outside at dusk and Heir reached out and brushed the back of his hand down

Treasa's cheek. They both looked so happy and so much in love.

Shianne felt tears welling up in her eyes and she sniffled.

"Now you are sad." Aris sounded sad too. He hooked his finger under her chin and tilted her head back so that they were looking at each other.

"I just thought about my father and my step-mother and how happy they were." A puzzled expression crossed Aris's face and she explained. "Before Val, he was married to Treasa. She was the mother to my younger brothers and sisters. He loved her very much and she died." A tear escaped.

Aris brushed his thumb across her cheek, taking her tear. "It is," he searched for the word, "difficult to lose those we love."

Suddenly, Shianne was finding it hard to breathe. She'd known she liked Aris. She liked how he looked, of course. She couldn't say she was only human, but the phrase was appropriate when it came to the appreciation of his god-like beauty. It wasn't just that, though. He wasn't just man-candy to sit around and stare at. He was intelligent and funny and sweet...

Damnit.

She *really* liked Aris. Liked him in a way that could turn into something more.

Panic flooded her and she took a step back, moving behind his reach. She bent and picked a flower to pretend that she had just gotten the whim rather than not wanting him to touch her. She didn't even know if he was thinking the same thing, but she couldn't take the chance. She glanced at him out of the corner of her eye, dreading his reaction.

He had remained standing where he was, watching her with undisguised admiration. He didn't look like he was upset with her abrupt movement. Not angry or hurt. Just calm. He looked like the same kind Aris with whom she had spent many hours talking and laughing since she came to the island.

"We're leaving tomorrow," she blurted out. She wasn't sure why she said it. Maybe to remind herself that whatever this was with Aris would end as soon as she stepped on that plane. A relationship with a human was ludicrous, but a long-distance one even more so.

Aris nodded. "And we go with you."

Shianne stared at him. She couldn't have heard correctly. Her grandmother never left the island.

"Rupa and I go with you." Aris smiled widely, leaving no doubt as to what he meant.

"That's – that's great," Shianne stammered. On one level, she really meant it. Her family would be ecstatic to have Rupa with them, and she would definitely enjoy spending more time with Aris. But that was also the reason she was absolutely petrified at the thought of Rupa and her human coming to Paris.

Shianne smiled, but it was a hollow smile. All of the earlier levity she'd felt with Aris was turning into panic, carefully hidden behind a polite mask. She couldn't fall for a human. She knew better. She'd been through it once and that had been enough. She hadn't even wanted to become friends with Val, but that had at least worked out. If she let herself care about Aris, really care about him, it could only end one way. Her heart broken into a thousand pieces.

And yet, as she walked back up the path next to him, she couldn't stop the little voice in the back of her head from wondering if it might not be worth it.

CHAPTER FIFTEEN

Mid-November weather in Paris was perfect, Alexander thought. Gray and cold, it looked exactly how he felt. The weather did anyway. The bright and bustling shops decked out for Christmas definitely didn't reflect his mood. Every time he passed someone calling out holiday greetings, he pretended he hadn't been fluent in French since Napoleon had been elected president. He'd chosen French for his foreign language because of the Frenchman. He'd liked the way the man dressed.

He trudged along behind the rest of his family as they headed to the fourth salon they'd visited since arriving in Paris five days ago. Shianne's Vamp Tramp Sprays were apparently making quite the wave among the Parisian community. The first unveiling had drawn a respectable crowd. Now, the Vamps couldn't leave their hotel without being mobbed. Well, he amended, more accurately, Shianne couldn't leave without the people flocking to her. The rest of them were recognized, but she was definitely the belle of the ball here in Paris.

Not that he cared. Alexander hunched his shoulders and shoved his hands more deeply into his pockets. The cold didn't bother him, but it gave him the excuse not to walk tall and straight. He didn't have the energy to pretend that everything was fine all the time. It was exhausting enough to do it when his family was paying attention.

Someone jostled him and it took all of his self-control not to snap at them. And he didn't mean snap in the sense of a verbal lashing. He meant fangs out, cutting into flesh.

"I am sorry."

A heavily accented male voice caught his attention.

Alexander looked up at Aris who was smiling apologetically down at him.

"The..." Aris frowned as he gestured at the snow-covered ground, obviously searching for a word.

"Snow?" Alexander supplied. He straightened. "Ice?"

Aris's face lit up. "Yes. Ice. The ice slipped."

Alexander half-smiled. "I think you mean the ice was slippery."

Aris nodded. "Yes. I am still working to speak English. The ice was slippery." He carefully repeated what Alexander had said.

"You're doing quite well," Alexander said. He leaned closer to Aris, brushing his arm against the other man's.

The emptiness inside his chest gave a throb, as if he needed reminding that it was there. Wasn't that why he was flirting with Aris? To make the pain stop? Or at least make it fade to the back of his mind for even a short while? The idea of being able to turn Aris away from a woman was tempting, far more tempting than any challenge had been so far.

"Thank you," Aris said. He looked up ahead of them, not seeming to notice Alexander's proximity. "Your sister is good teacher."

The lust Alexander had been trying to kindle went out as ice water ran through him. He stepped away from Aris, horrified at what he'd been considering. As the human hurried back up to where Shianne was walking, Alexander berated himself. Was he really that far gone that he'd try to seduce the man his sister cared for just to satiate his own desire?

He ran his hand through his hair. The disgust and disappointment he'd seen in Noah's eyes was justified. If he couldn't put his own sister above himself, he didn't deserve any sort of happiness, no matter how brief. He deserved to be miserable, to do penance for all that he'd done. And still, he found himself looking for something, anything, that could ease the pain inside him, warm the chill that had nothing to do with the weather.

He pressed his hand against his chest, over his slow-beating heart. He'd thought that after three weeks, he would be over Noah. After all, he'd never had any problem getting over anyone before. Then again, he'd never been dumped before. He'd always been the one who'd set the terms of the relationship, if what he'd had with others over the centuries could be considered relationships. Moving on hadn't really been an issue because he'd always gone into an encounter knowing that he would be finding someone else not too much later. He'd lived in the moment, never thinking of anything other than the slip and slide of bodies, the pleasure and the blood.

He made a growling sound that should have shocked him out of his dark mood. Instead, it just reminded him of what he didn't have and what he wanted. He glanced up towards the others and confirmed that no one was watching. He slipped into one of the stores and waited for the crowds and reporters to follow his family, leaving him free to wander on his own.

Movement to his right caught his eye and he turned his head. Maybe he didn't need to wander after all.

The young man staring at him had large, dark eyes, like two liquid pools of chocolate and thick black hair. He was thin with a nose a bit too big for his face, but he also had the look of someone who wasn't quite done growing, so the rest of him might catch up in the next year or so. Alexander ran his eyes slowly over the young man's body, from his head to his feet and then back up again. One of the things he loved about Europe. Barely legal here was different than back home. Noah had been close to that cut off point. Alexander judged this one to be seventeen or eighteen, older than France's age of consent and not so young that he, at nineteen, felt like he was robbing the cradle.

He crossed to the Parisian and held out his hand in a wordless invitation.

"*Je suis Pierre.*" His voice was deeper than Alexander had

expected.

"Alexander." He glanced around the shop he'd entered. It was apparently a candy store, and judging by the apron Pierre was wearing, it was his place of employment. "That's enough pleasantries, don't you think?" He used one of his favorite French sentences. "*Allons-nous aller quelque part privée?*"

Pink stained Pierre's cheeks as he nodded. He didn't need any additional coaxing to pull Alexander towards the back of the store. He called over his shoulder to the amused looking elderly woman at the cash register, telling her he was taking his lunch break.

The store room was dark and smelled of cinnamon and chocolate. Alexander may not have been able to eat human food, but that didn't mean he disliked the smells. Chocolate and cinnamon happened to be two that he liked quite a bit. Before the door had shut behind them, he had his hands around Pierre's waist and was shoving him back against the solid wooden door.

His mouth pressed against the younger man's lips hard enough to elicit a pained sound mingled with a moan. Pierre's hands were all over him as he eagerly returned the kiss. Alexander spun the dark-haired boy around and began to kiss the back of his neck. Pierre sighed, pushing back against Alexander. The vampire easily held Pierre in place with one arm as the other one made the necessary adjustments to their clothing to get him in the position he wanted, naked and accessible.

It was rough and fast, full of pained whimpers mixed with moans of pleasure, each one equally exciting to Alexander. He pulled at the skin on the side of Pierre's neck, feeling the blood pumping beneath the surface. His fingers curled in Pierre's hair, pulling the young man's head to the side. He didn't ask permission or warn that it was coming. His teeth sank into the soft flesh and he felt Pierre begin to struggle as the hot, copper liquid filled his mouth.

****

Pru loved that her grandmother had come with them. Rupa seemed to understand her in a way the others couldn't. She was...well, she was more like how Pru had always thought her mother would've been. Taylor Ann was enjoying herself even though the tabloids were still throwing out the occasional accusation about her relationship with Stephen. Shianne and Aris were rarely apart and Pru was beginning to suspect that her eldest sister might be interested in more than the man-toy's good looks. Not that Pru could blame her. Aris was really nice. He didn't talk much to her, but when he did, he wasn't condescending. She liked that.

Things should have been great. But they weren't.

Pru stuck her hands in her pockets as she walked between her father and her grandmother. Heir had never been a real talker, but he'd been unusually quiet ever since he and Alexander had gotten to Greece. Erickson had too. Pru was starting to worry that something was really wrong. Usually, Shianne and Erickson were joined at the hip unless apart for one of their little trysts or on a business venture. If things had been normal, Shianne would've been walking with Erickson and Aris, flirting with the human while still carrying on a conversation with her brother. Instead, Erickson was slinking along behind Di, looking like someone had just killed his cat or something. Or, since he didn't have a cat and probably wouldn't have really cared about it getting killed if he did, he looked like someone had made fun of his fangs. He was awfully sensitive about them.

Pru had tried figuring out what was wrong with her oldest brother, even going online to see what the rumors were, but that hadn't helped. Most of the stories were still about Alexander and Noah, the rest about the Vamps' trip and a couple about Taylor Ann and her doctor. That had been last week though. Maybe she needed to check again.

She sighed. She'd been trying to avoid the stories about Alexander and Noah. They just made her sad. She'd known about the break-up before the media had caught wind of it, but she'd been holding out hope that Alexander could fix whatever he'd done. She liked the way Noah was with him, and the human had actually been a good match for her bed-hopping brother.

Speaking of...

Pru looked over her shoulder and frowned. Alexander had been right behind them, but he wasn't there now. She stopped, turning around completely and scanning the crowd that was following them at a respectful distance. Darius had gotten a bit physical with a couple overzealous reporters yesterday, so everyone was keeping back to prevent a repeat.

"Prussia?" Rupa said her name.

"Where's Alexander?" Pru asked. She didn't want to get her brother in trouble, but she'd been uneasy about him for a few days now. He seemed less and less like himself, and she was worried.

"He came with us, did he not?" It was Heir speaking now, but Pru didn't look up at him either.

"Yeah, and he was back there the last time I looked," Pru said.

"When was that?" Rupa asked.

Pru thought for a moment. "About fifteen minutes ago."

"I'm sure he just saw something he wanted to buy," Heir said.

Her father's voice sounded nonchalant, but Pru could hear something underneath it. He was worried too, she realized. That made sense. He'd been in London when everything smelly had hit the fan. Maybe that's what had been bothering her dad, his concern for Alexander. It still didn't explain Erickson though...

"There he is," Rupa said suddenly.

Pru glanced up to catch where her grandmother was pointing and followed the line of sight. Sure enough, coming around the corner with his usual swagger was her favorite brother. The knot in Pru's chest eased some when she saw him striding towards them. He looked like he was feeling better already. That was good. She smiled at him as he approached and he returned the grin, flashing blood-stained fangs.

Pru's eyes widened slightly and she turned to hurry after her grandmother. She didn't want her face giving away that she'd seen that Alexander had fed. The camera crew was focusing most of their attention on Taylor Ann and Shianne with their humans, so chances were no one else would catch the blood. That was a good thing. They were still supposed to be doing the family meal time on camera thing that they'd started back home. Their dad would be furious if he found out Alexander had eaten.

And that also raised the question: who had he drunk from? All of the humans they were feeding from while in Paris were back at the hotel. Only Aris was out with them, and he only fed Rupa. The rest of the Vamps made due with the people Di had hired. If Alexander had picked up some random person – some random man – and fed from him, they needed to make sure no one found out.

Pru swore silently. She'd been having such a good time and looking forward to Christmas in Edinburgh. She'd never been to her father's birthplace. Why did her brothers have to pick now to start acting like ass-hats? Granted, Erickson always could be a total douche, but never so that it spoiled the fun. If anything, he didn't know how to take anything seriously. And Leo was just being typical loner Leo, preferring to be locked in a room with stacks and stacks of dusty books. But Alexander never would've done anything to jeopardize something he knew she'd been looking forward to for months. She needed to figure out a way to snap him out of his post-Noah funk or he was going to ruin Christmas.

CHAPTER SIXTEEN

"You're actually excited about going to the ballet?" Val couldn't conceal her shock. At least, her voice couldn't. Her face was more expressionless than usual. She'd seen a few worry lines that morning and had Dr. Darcy give her a few injections to take care of the problem. She liked to get ahead of things whenever she could.

"Just because I don't like fluffy tutus doesn't mean I don't like good stories, music and appreciate the athleticism of dance." Pru lifted her chin and crossed her arms over her chest.

Val was thankful she couldn't smile at the moment. She understood Pru's posturing. The girl was known for being a tomboy and hating anything even remotely girly. She was the complete opposite of her sisters. Ballet was another thing that society said was feminine and Pru didn't want anyone to think that was why she liked it.

"All right, all right." Val held up her hands in surrender. "But, you do know that you have to dress up to go, right? This isn't some community theater thing. This is the newest ballet in Paris, and it's being held at their oldest theater."

"I know." Pru nodded. "Grandmother took me shopping yesterday for it."

If Rupa could get Pru to dress up without the littlest Vamp throwing a fit, more power to her, Val thought. She loved her stepchildren, but they could all be difficult in their own ways. Pru was the one Val found the most difficult, but not because Pru was generally badly behaved. Val just didn't understand her. Then again, Val had been born in a time where being a woman had meant marrying and having a family. Respectable females always wore dresses and did as their elders told them. While Val appreciated the strides in women's rights over the decades, and believed women should be allowed to dress as they wished and be equal to men, she just didn't understand ones like Pru who didn't like all of the things Val had grown up being told were what women wanted.

"Val," Pru hesitated, like she wanted to ask something but wasn't sure she was allowed.

"Yes, Dear?" Val sat on the edge of the bed.

"Is-is everything okay?"

Val would've given Pru a puzzled look if she'd been able to make any kind of expression. As it was, she just had to rely on words. "Of course. Why wouldn't it be?"

Pru pulled her feet up onto the bed and hugged her knees. The expression on her face was so young that one almost could've forgotten that she was old enough that she'd learned to read from a first edition of Hans Christian Anderson's fairy tales – purchased just days after it had been published. She may have looked and behaved like a twelve year-old, but she'd seen enough history that there were times she seemed much closer to almost two centuries-old than to twelve. This, however, was not one of those times.

"Pru, why would you think something's wrong?" Val asked, putting her hand on Pru's back and making small, soothing circles. When Pru had been a toddler, the only way anyone could get her to nap was to rub her back like that.

Pru shrugged, her eyes fixed on her bedspread. Val knew something was bothering her step-daughter, but she also knew if she forced it, Pru would never open up.

"If you don't want to say, that's okay," Val said. "But just remember that I'm here whenever you do want to talk."

Pru nodded. Her eyes darted up to Val's face, then back down to her bed again. "Thank you," she said.

Val waited for a few more minutes before standing, wanting to be sure Pru didn't want to say anything now. She started for the door when Pru's voice stopped her.

"Will you do my hair tonight?"

Val's eyes widened, giving her the closest to a surprised expression she could manage at the moment. She was careful to keep her voice even though. "Of course. I'll come by at six. Will that be okay?"

"Yeah. Thanks."

Val left, hurrying off to find Shianne. She was fine when it came to the latest fashions for women, but she didn't know the best style to give Pru and she didn't want to mess it up. That tangled mess that was Pru's hair sometimes seemed to have a mind of its own. If she did something stupid, Pru would probably just do what she usually did and let the bright red locks go wild. Val had a feeling Rupa wouldn't like that very much.

****

Leo would have preferred to stay at the house the Vamps had rented for their stay in Paris, and his father might not have even noticed, preoccupied as he was with this Erickson situation, but Leo did not wish to do anything that drew attention to him at the moment. He'd been checking out art galleries and museums all over the city since the Vamps had arrived, often asking family members to come along to allay suspicions. He had not yet found anything and, again, he was running out of time. His moves must become more bold, he knew, and yet that would risk his father discovering what he was looking for. He hoped that by attending the ballet, his father would be led to believe that Leo's excursions into the city were only additional immersion into the city's artistic history and culture.

"Hot damn, Leo. You clean up nice," Shianne teased good-naturedly as Leo entered the parlor where most of the rest of the Vamp family was waiting.

Leo gave her an exasperated, but fond look. While he did not understand it, and even to some extent felt human-vampire relationships were wrong, he did enjoy seeing his sister happy as she spent time with Aris. He fidgeted in his modern suit. He had never been one to pay attention to fashion trends and generally wore whatever Di purchased for him, so he did not know if this was the most fashionable suit, but if Shianne thought it looked nice, then he would take her word for it. Although, he thought, the matter of his appearance was hardly something with which he was concerned. As long as he did not reflect poorly on the Vamp name, he was satisfied

Leo could feel everyone looking at him and he squirmed under their gazes. He knew they were only reacting to Shianne's statement regarding his attire, but he felt a surprising flare of guilt. For the first time, it occurred to him that perhaps one or more of his siblings might also wish to know what he had found. They, after all, had also loved his mother.

"Treasa."

Leo started at his father's soft exhalation, certain that, somehow, Heir knew of Leo's findings. Then he saw that no one was looking at him. All eyes were turned towards the entrance to the parlor. He did the same and heard himself gasp.

The figure was tall and slender with luminous green eyes. She wore a long green and silver dress made of a shimmery material for which he had no name. Her hair was piled on her head, gleaming in the light like flames.

For a moment, he was pulled back in time to his childhood, and he took a step forward, a hand squeezing around his heart. "Mama?" The word was the whisper of a child, barely even audible to his own ears.

"Yes, I'm wearing a dress. Let's not all have a conniption over it." Pru's voice shattered the image.

"Prussia, my darling," Rupa recovered first. "You are quite stunning." She stepped forward and took Pru's hands. She kissed both of Pru's cheeks. "The very image of your mother."

Leo's throat was tight. He had not realized what it would be like to see his sister looking so much like their mother. He had caught glimpses before, but this was so much more. Looking at the others told him that he was not the only one who had been shocked, not by the fact that Pru was dressed up, but rather that she had appeared as if Treasa Vamp had returned to them.

Di broke the still tense silence. "We should be going. It wouldn't do for us to show up late."

Leo saw the others nodding, but he was not sure he could move. The family began to move towards the exit but he still could not bring himself to walk after them. He felt a hand on his arm and he looked down to see Taylor Ann.

"I saw her too," she said softly. "I never knew just how much Pru looked like her."

He could see tears glistening in her eyes and, for the first time, he was forced to acknowledge that he was not the only one who felt the loss of his mother...of their mother. He could not find the words to tell her all that he was feeling, but her fingers tightened around his arm and he knew that she understood all without him having to say a word.

"Let's go," Taylor Ann said.

She reached down and took his hand. They walked out that way, hand in hand as if they were still small and young.

The ride to the ballet was quiet, though Rupa attempted to fill the silence with bits of history about the theater. Leo did not hear any of it. Taylor Ann still held his hand, but he did not look at her either. He stared out the window, lost in the past. He was so wrapped up that he almost missed when they arrived at their destination. As the others climbed out of the limo, he pulled himself out of his thoughts and turned to follow them. He wanted nothing more than to return to the house and lose himself in the pain that was starting to creep in, but he could not. Not yet.

To provide himself with a distraction more than actually wanting to know, he turned to his grandmother and asked, "What ballet are we seeing?"

She made a face of distaste as she answered, "It's a modern classical blend, a new take on *Alice in Wonderland*, called *Edge of the Rabbit Hole*."

Leo was now regretting having agreed to come. He had never been a fan of Lewis Carroll. He had met Charles Dodgson once and found the author to be slightly disturbing.

"Apparently your network has invested in this show which is why we are being required to attend." Rupa sounded amused. "I would have preferred something more refined."

As the music began and the lights came up on the surreal set, Leo thought to agree with his grandmother at first. Then Aliz came onto the stage and he was mesmerized. Her slender body held all of the strength and grace that a ballerina needed. Unlike the other dancers who wore their hair up, hers tumbled around her shoulders like a dark wave, and flew away from her as she leaped and spun. From where they sat in the front row, he was able to see the intricate details of the gold and red mask that covered the top half of her face, and he had a sudden longing to see what lay beneath the mask. Her eyes were dark as well, and as she passed by, they met his for the briefest of moments.

Everything that had been plaguing him since that moment when his childhood shattered faded into the background. He saw no one else, heard only the music of her movements. He understood now that there were some things stronger than the pull of the past, than the need for answers and revenge. He understood the sadness he saw in Alexander, the longing on Shianne's face. Human or vampire, he did not care. He could feel the pull towards this beautiful stranger, feel the pain and heartbreak in her dance. Her Aliz was not the child of the stories, but a young woman who had experienced much in her short life.

Time seemed to stand still as he watched her. Then, as Aliz woke to find herself in Twonderland, she reached towards her mask and Leo held his breath. He let it out in a rush as the dancer revealed a delicate face. Exquisite bone structure and pale, flawless skin. His stomach twisted in a way that it had not done before. She was vampire.

And she was perfect.

****

Pru had taken the seat between Leo and Rupa, not wanting distractions from any of her other family, but then she'd seen Leo's face when the ballerina playing Aliz came out onto the stage. For the first few minutes, she'd been amused, thinking that her brother was actually enjoying the ballet. Then, as she'd started watching him more than the performers, she realized that he wasn't actually following the story. His eyes moved with Aliz, never leaving her, not even when another character took the spotlight to lead Aliz into Twonderland.

He was watching Aliz, Pru thought with a shock. And it wasn't an appreciation of the young woman's art form either. Pru had seen that expression before. On Alexander's face when he was with Noah, and more recently, it had been creeping onto Shianne's when she talked to Aris. The one person she'd never thought she'd see staring at someone with that look of complete fascination was Leo. Especially when it wasn't clear if the girl was human or vampire.

Until the mask came off.

Pru saw it on Leo's face even before she looked up at the stage. The dancer was one of them and Leo was completely enraptured.

As the first act progressed, she found herself dividing her attention between the ballet and her brother. She'd never seen him like this before. His eyes were wide as he leaned forward slightly, as if his entire body was tuned to the girl. As the final scene of the act began, Pru leaned over to her grandmother.

"What do you know about the lead?"

Rupa answered in a soft murmur that only Pru could hear. "Only what the program tells me. Her name is Saraleti and she is eighteen. She joined the company last year and comes from a small town in the south of France. Whether she is Turned or Settled, I cannot tell, nor do I know her true age."

"None of the others are like us, are they?" Pru asked.

Rupa shook her head. "And I do not believe any of them know what she is." She had a thoughtful expression on her face. "I once knew every vampire in Paris, but that time has long since passed. We are scattered. Even as humans use their technology to connect more, we lose our connection as a people."

Pru gave her grandmother a puzzled look. She may have been older than any human, but she was still very young by vampire standards. There were some things that couldn't be understood until four or five centuries had passed. And Pru sometimes wondered if even then she'd feel the same way about the rest of her kind as Rupa, Heir and even Di felt. Her grandmother was right about one thing. Vampires weren't in contact very often. Aside from her family, Pru had probably only met two or three vampires in her lifetime, and they had been friends of her father's who had come to visit. She knew what she was and didn't try to deny it, but she also felt as if she had a place among the humans.

A place to belong. That really was what it was all about, Pru thought. All of them wanted that as much as humans did. It was why Taylor Ann had nearly killed herself with those stupid capsules and why Shianne and Erickson basically whored themselves to the camera. It was what Alexander was looking for all those times he brought random men home and why losing Noah was killing him.

When the lights came up for intermission, Pru decided that even though she couldn't figure out what was wrong with Erickson or fix things with Noah for Alexander, she could do something for Leo. She excused herself and headed for one of the people who looked like they were there in an official capacity. She knew one of the cameramen was following her and hoped that, this time, things would work to her advantage.

"*Bonjour*," she said as she smiled at the middle-aged man standing by the exit. "English?" Her smile widened when he nodded. That was good. She only knew half a dozen phrases in French, and only two of them were ones she'd use in polite conversation. "My name is Prussia Vamp."

"Ah, *House of Vamp*." The man's eyes lit up. That was very good.

"Yes." She nodded. "We're here in Paris filming our television show and I came to see this wonderful ballet."

The cameraman snickered softly and Pru glared at him over her shoulder, flashing enough fang to make him go pale. She smiled as she turned back to the man by the exit. "Here's the thing," she said.

"My brother, Leo, he'd really like to meet Saraleti. Is there any possible way you could make that happen?" She batted her eyes at him, wishing she had her brothers' powers of persuasion. All she had to work with was looking like a cute little kid trying to help out her brother.

Fortunately, it worked. Less than ten minutes later, she was heading back to her seat, humming happily.

"So," she announced as she reached her family. "I just got us all invited backstage to meet the dancers after the show."

Leo didn't say a word, but Pru saw his already startling blue eyes brighten until they almost looked like they were glowing. She grinned. That was what she wanted to see. Her family, happy.

CHAPTER SEVENTEEN

Of all the idioms and clichés that had evolved over the years, none confused Leo more than ones intended to describe love. Butterflies in the stomach. Heart about to burst. Head spinning. Falling head over heels. None of these things had ever made sense to him until the moment he stepped backstage and saw Saraleti sitting at her make-up table, pulling her thick hair back from her face. He got it then. All of it. The nerves at not knowing what to say. The dread of not knowing how she would receive him. There was a knot in his stomach and it was becoming increasingly difficult to breathe.

"Relax." Pru's voice came from his side but he did not look down at her. "I don't have a lot of experience in this area, but I'm pretty sure you want to play it cool."

Now he did look down. "Play it cool?"

Pru smiled up at him. "Look, I'm only going to say this once, so you better appreciate it." She put her hand on his shoulder.

"You've got manners straight out of a Jane Austen novel, the whole mysterious angst thing that's so in right now, and you look like one of those guys from the CW."

He stared at her. He had not understood anything after Jane Austen and did not know if any of what his sister had said was positive.

Pru sighed, apparently figuring out why he still looked confused. "Don't sell yourself short. Go talk to her. She's going to like you."

Leo desperately hoped that this would be true. He allowed Pru to give him a gentle push in Saraleti's direction. He approached the dancer with a shy smile on his face. He had never spoken to a female vampire who was not related to him.

"*Bonjour*," he said softly.

She looked up at him, a guarded expression on her face.

"*Mon nom est* Leo." He held out his hand, palm up rather than to the side. One did not shake hands with someone such as Saraleti. "*C'est un plaisir de vous rencontrer.*"

Surprise flitted across her eyes, though he did not know if it was from him speaking French or from the hand in front of her. She slid her hand into his, her palm cool and dry. He bent over it and pressed his lips against the back of her hand.

"You are American?" she asked in lightly accented, but flawless English.

"I am," Leo nodded. His ancestry may have come from Scotland, but he had always considered himself American. A vampire, yes, but his nationality was American.

"What brings you to Paris?" she asked as she took her hand back.

Leo felt a pang of sadness at the loss. "My family." He gestured behind him to where the other Vamps were talking to the rest of the company and trying not to look as if they were watching him. The ever-present cameraman was just a few feet away. He motioned to that next. "We are filming a television show." He hoped it did not sound as if he was bragging. The last thing he wanted was for Saraleti to believe he wished for fame. "It was not my decision."

A small smile played at her lips, sending a thrill through Leo. He had never imagined that something that trivial could elicit such a reaction from him.

Saraleti stood. She was close to Taylor Ann's height, putting her within just a few inches of Leo's own. She looked at him with unveiled curiosity, her eyes narrowing after a moment. "You are...like me."

He nodded. "We are vampire." He paused, then asked, "Do you mind if I ask when you were born?"

For a moment, he did not think she would answer, but after a brief hesitation, she did. Her words were clipped, as if this was not a subject on which she wanted to speak. "I was born during the *Belle Époque*."

Leo recognized that phrase. It was a term used to describe France from 1871 until the First World War. That would make

Saraleti a little over a century old, depending on when during those forty years she had been born. He also knew that meant she'd been Turned. He had never heard of a vampire who had aged to eighteen in just a century. Surprisingly, he did not care that she had once been human. For a moment, he wondered if he would have cared if she had still been human, but he pushed that thought aside. Such was not the case and posturing questions would not make it so.

"Leo," Shianne called to him. "We're all going to take a walk before going back to the house."

He turned slightly to see his eldest sister smiling at him.

"Would you like to ask your new friend to join us?"

Leo turned back towards Saraleti. He had never been more nervous, but he refused to give in to the anxiety that she would say no. If he did not ask, he would never know, and that would haunt him as so much of the unknown already did.

"Would you like to walk with us?" he asked. He could hear the waver in his voice and hoped that she would not.

Slowly, she nodded. "I believe I would like that very much."

****

"Shianne!"

"Shianne!"

"Miss Vamp!"

She'd never thought she'd actually be tired of hearing her name being shouted by reporters and fans, but it was starting to wear on her. She smiled and waved as the Vamps left the theater, but a part of her wondered what it would be like to be able to come to something like this and not need Darius and half a dozen muscle-bound men to keep back the people who wanted to mob her. At least, she thought, it was a good kind of mobbing. No pitchforks or torches.

She could hear people calling out for other members of her family as well, though her name was the loudest. Still, she heard the brief pause the instant Saraleti walked out alongside Leo, and then the shouts for those two almost equaled the ones for her. Still, the Parisians seemed to love her insatiably.

"They adore you here," Aris said as he fell into step next to her.

It was strange, Shianne thought, how naturally the two of them walked together. She and Erickson had a rhythm at which they walked and talked, as did she and Val, but the latter had come only after decades together. With Aris, it had been almost instantaneous.

"They do," she agreed. She smiled at a group of fans holding up a sign that said: *Nous vous aimons,* Shianne. She gave them a wave and called, "*Je t'aime aussi!*"

"You do not seem as pleased with the attention as you once were." Aris spoke in Greek to get the full sentence out without stumbling.

Shianne's smile faltered. "I'm not," she admitted. She glanced over at her shoulder at the camera pointed at her. She switched to her own poor Greek. "It is a little too much."

Aris brushed his fingers down Shianne's arm. "Then why do you not quit?"

"It's not that easy," she said, changing back to English.

Silence fell between them as they continued to walk. Shianne had never felt like this before. She'd always wanted to be the center of attention, so much so that she'd quickly learned that if she and Erickson shared the spotlight, neither one of them ever had to be out of it. She thought back over the centuries and realized that she'd never once had the desire to be alone.

Although, she amended, she didn't exactly want to be alone right now either. No, she thought. What she wanted was to be able to be somewhere quiet with Aris. Someplace the two of them could talk completely openly without having to worry about who was listening or what the cameras would hear. She wondered if there were things he wouldn't say with the cameras around. She knew there certainly were for her.

It was strange, she thought, that after so much time clamoring to be famous, she would want to take a break from it just when things were peaking. She'd seen celebrities do it all the time over the centuries. They'd burn themselves out on whatever their field was and then it'd be a downward spiral, rehab or jail, and then a comeback after a short span of "finding themselves." She'd always thought that because she wasn't human, she wouldn't burn out like they did, but here she was, wishing that her fans would leave her in peace for even just a few minutes.

She just hoped that didn't mean jail was coming next. There was no way she could pull off Day-Glo orange.

****

Pru was still chattering excitedly when the limo pulled up in front of the villa. She'd been completely entranced by the sets and the ballerinas, and Erickson suspected she had something to do with the lead joining them. He'd watched Leo with the girl – Saraleti, he believed her name was – and was struck for the first time by how much Leo looked like him. Seeing his littlest brother walking alongside a beautiful girl had really taken Erickson back. When, he wondered, had he gone from the enjoyment of the little things, the slow seduction of a woman, enjoying the chase? When had it become just about the conquest itself, the physical act of two bodies, the rush and taste of blood? He couldn't remember the last time he'd actually pursued a woman rather than moving on if she didn't succumb in a short enough period of time. And wasn't that what had gotten him into his current predicament?

As the Vamps climbed out of the limo, Heir caught Erickson's eye and nodded. Erickson nodded back, his stomach clenching. He waited until Di approached each of the cameramen, speaking quietly to them until they got a glazed look in their eyes. When the last one had lowered his camera, Erickson cleared his throat. No one seemed to notice so he tried speaking. "Hey, um, everyone."

All eyes turned to him and the cameras followed. He swallowed hard. "I need to talk to everyone, so if we can all go to the main room..."

He saw curiosity and confusion on everyone's faces except the three who knew, and strangely enough, Leo. Normally, he would've thought that it was just because Leo was in his own little world like usual, but his brother's gaze was sharp tonight. Erickson shook his head and followed the others into the front room. Everyone found a seat and then turned to look at him, waiting.

Erickson's stomach was in knots. What was he supposed to do? Just blurt it out? He looked at his father but Heir's face was blank, not giving him any idea of what he was supposed to do. His gaze slid over one to Di, but her expression was just as unreadable as his father's. He turned to Shianne next and she shrugged. Apparently, she didn't know what to say either. He felt a flare of anger towards the human standing next to Shianne. His sister was supposed to be here with him, supporting him, not flirting with their grandmother's "assistant."

"So, um." Erickson shuffled his feet, praying that someone would take pity on him and share the news so he didn't have to. No one did though and he knew they were getting impatient. He took a deep breath and decided to plunge right in. "I know most of you saw those rumors about that pop star, Tedi, and me before we left the States." He forced himself to raise his head. "Well, not all of it was rumor." One of his sisters made a noise like a gasp, but he couldn't tell if it was Taylor Ann or Pru. "She's pregnant. The baby's mine."

CHAPTER EIGHTEEN

The silence that followed was the kind of absolute quiet that could only come in a roomful of vampires. Only the sounds of Aris's and Stephen's very human heartbeats could be heard for nearly a full minute.

And then came the explosion as everyone talked at once.

"You got Tedi pregnant?!" Pru exclaimed, leaping to her feet.

"How is that possible?" Taylor Ann asked her father.

"What are you going to do?" Rupa asked.

"Can't believe it took this long for it to happen." Alexander's comment earned a glare from his brother.

Heir held up his hands and everyone quieted. He had expected their reactions, though he was disappointed with his middle son's snark. The only one who surprised him was Leo who didn't appear to be surprised at all, and was also not being vocal. He'd thought for sure his youngest son would have something to say on the matter.

"Most human-vampire offspring are the result of a vampire who has not Settled and a human, and even those are not common," Heir explained. "Even more rare are the instances where procreation has occurred between a Settled male vampire and a human female. While a Settled female vampire no longer has the ability to bear children, a Settled male may still retain the necessary...biology for reproduction."

Everyone stared at him. He knew this was news to them. It wasn't common knowledge, even among vampires, and he disliked the discussion of personal matters enough that he had avoided speaking of these things unless absolutely necessary. Unfortunately, Erickson had made it necessary.

Di picked up where he left off. "A DNA test confirmed that Erickson is the father of Tedi's child. Ms. Mitchell will be sent on a vacation for the duration of her pregnancy, at the end of which, the baby will be brought to live with us. We are quashing the rumors in the press as being just that as we do not yet know how we want to spin the story."

"Is she going to live with us too?" Pru interrupted.

"No," Di said. "Ms. Mitchell has agreed to sign away her rights to the child."

"She's going to give away her baby?" Taylor Ann asked softly.

Heir looked down at his middle daughter, puzzled. She'd never expressed an interest in children before. His eyes darted to the therapist next to her. He hoped that those rumors were false. Taylor Ann was delicate. She didn't need a romantic entanglement any time soon.

"She has agreed that we are better fit to raise a human-vampire child," Di answered.

Heir saw Stephen open his mouth as if he wanted to ask a question, but then shut it again. If the human had spoken, Heir probably would've ignored him, but because he'd realized that it wasn't his place, Heir would allow the questions he knew the young man was dying to ask.

"Stephen, did you want to know something?"

"I've never heard of a half-human, half-vampire," the doctor said slowly. "Outside of fiction, of course. These children, are they...mortal?"

To everyone's surprise, it was Rupa who answered, "Very little is known about the human-vampire hybrid. As my son said, they are rare. The last I remember was a set of twins born in," she paused and looked to Di. "The seventeen twenties?"

Di shook her head. "Those weren't humanpires. Alphonse had been Turned just after Eloise conceived, she wasn't Turned until after the children were born. The children grew as humans and then chose to remain mortal"

Rupa nodded. "You are correct. Then it was Jocelyn and Albert in the fifteen nineties."

Di nodded. "Jocelyn was an Unsettled vampire, Albert human. They had a little girl."

"And Bree and Declan, their son was born shortly before Heir, isn't that right?" Rupa asked.

Di nodded again. "I helped birth him myself. Declan was an Unsettled vampire and Bree human. I have never personally known of a Settled vampire and a human procreating."

"So the babies were fine?"

Heir had almost forgotten why the women were reminiscing about the past.

Di and Rupa exchanged glances and it was Di who answered the question. "They were both completely healthy."

"But were they human or vampire?" Stephen asked. His cheeks were red as if he was embarrassed by his question.

"They were both," Rupa said. "A humanpire can survive on either blood or human food. In fact, they need both until..." Her voice trailed off.

"Until what?" Pru asked, her eyes round. She knew human-vampire hybrids were possible, but they'd never discussed the specifics.

"Humanpires ages much more slowly than humans, but faster than natural born vampires," Heir said gently, knowing age was a sensitive subject with his youngest. "A humanpire may live for two or three centuries, but never stop aging and eventually die from old age. Or, they may Settle just as a natural born vampire does. There is no way to know until it happens."

He could see the horror in Pru's eyes. Not knowing when she would Settle was something she struggled with, but to not know IF it would happen would be so much worse.

"How's this going to work?" Shianne finally spoke up. "In case you haven't noticed, we're kinda in the public eye. We can't just have Di helping the crew forget what they were doing every time the baby cries."

Heir was impressed that his eldest daughter had thought that thoroughly about the situation. He had assumed she would be more concerned with things like shopping for the child. "We are discussing options," Heir said. "That is one of the reasons we are concealing Ms. Mitchell's pregnancy."

"One of the reasons?" Alexander asked sharply.

Heir gave his son a concerned look. There was a hostility radiating off of Alexander that was new and disturbing. How had he missed this?

"Yes," Di answered the question. "As this baby will be the first humanpire the human world has known, there are bound to be hate groups who will want to hurt the child, as well as the human responsible. And, of course, you can't rule out all of the people who would pay a lot of money to have a half-human, half-vampire baby. Even with her fame and resources, Tedi would never be able to protect herself, let alone a baby, if word got out."

"So we're protecting her," Pru said. "Not just the baby."

"Correct," Heir said. He looked away from Alexander. "Now, we do have time. She's not due until May. Fortunately, human-vampire pregnancies are like pure-blood pregnancies and last nine months. The aging process doesn't begin slowing until after birth."

"That's probably why vampires and humans are able to procreate," Stephen mused. Everyone looked at him and his cheeks reddened. "Sorry, just thinking out loud."

Heir regarded the young man with a new appreciation. "I thought you were a psychologist."

Stephen nodded. "I am, but I did a secondary major in biology with a focus on genetics up through my Master's degree. I took the doctorate courses, but never completed my thesis."

Heir glanced at Di and saw that she was thinking the same thing he was. Di had been a nanny for years and would have no problem resuming the role, but it might be good to have a geneticist they could trust. He filed the information away for future reference. Now was not the time.

"We will be considering several scenarios over the next few months, but we will make sure all of you are included in the process as this is something that will not just be affecting one of us, but our entire family." Heir looked at his eldest son. "Is there anything you would like to add?"

Erickson shook his head.

"Very well," Heir said. "Shall we all retire so that our network friends can see we are through for the night?"

****

Leo lay awake in his bed, staring at the ceiling. His head was spinning. So many things had happened tonight. He had known of Erickson's child, but had not known much of these humanpires. He had also not foreseen that they would raise the child in their family. He found that the idea did not shock him as much as it once would have, even just yesterday. He saw nothing the same as he once had. Everything had changed the moment he had seen *her*.

Saraleti.

He sighed as he closed his eyes, picturing her face. He had never thought of faces beyond the symmetry of them, the familiarity of the ones he knew. The only one he had ever thought of in any sort of artistic or beautiful way was his mother, and that had been with a child's eye. With Saraleti, he could see the graceful line of her jaw, the elegance of her high cheekbones. She was beautiful, a work of art.

Her eyes were a deep, rich brown, the color of turned earth, and they had held such weight and sadness that, for the first time in his life, Leo felt the urge to hold someone and comfort them. He had not acted upon his desires as he did not yet know if his affections would be welcome. She was, after all, a stranger to him.

He did not wish her to be a stranger, he thought. Tomorrow, he had planned to venture into some of the more obscure art galleries in search of someone who knew about the sculpture with the mark, but that did not mean he needed to go alone. Having Saraleti with him would, in fact, make his father less suspicious of his motives, but that was not why Leo wanted to ask her to accompany him. He cared about finding his answers, but the thought of being able to spend more time with the beautiful ballerina made him happier than he had been in a very long time.

His finals thoughts were of her as he drifted off to sleep.

CHAPTER NINETEEN

Shianne knew that she had been awfully quiet as she and Aris made their way through the small shops, searching for possible Christmas presents for the family. It had taken them nearly a quarter of an hour to ditch the cameraman who'd been following them around all day, but when they had, they'd made their way to one of the most festive streets in the city. Shianne had been looking forward to this all week. She had actually purchased clothes just for this trip so that a bodyguard wouldn't be needed. Black pants, sturdy boots, a gray sweater and a bulky coat that was made more for warmth than appearance. Her hair was tucked up under a knit cap and a scarf obscured most of her face. Fortunately, it was cold enough that no one looked twice at how well she and Aris were bundled up.

She should have been ecstatic at being away from everyone and having Aris all to herself, but she couldn't pull herself out of her foul mood. And it was all *his* fault. Her stupid brother. The brother she'd always loved the most even though she knew she was supposed to love them all the same. The anger and bitterness had been growing ever since she'd heard the rumors, but she'd managed to push the negative emotions away by convincing herself that nothing she'd heard was true. Then when she'd found out it was, she'd been unable to stop the jealousy from bubbling up inside her. Staying away from him had helped, until last night.

"You want to go back?" Aris asked as he and Shianne ducked into an old bookstore.

She shook her head as she looked around. The place smelled musty, like dust and parchment and leather. She wrinkled her nose. She'd never been a big fan of books, especially not ones like these, but they were what Leo liked and she knew this was the place to find something for him. The place was empty save an ancient-looking man sitting next to an old-fashioned cash register, his chin on his chest, a gentle snore coming from his mouth. She began to walk towards the stacks furthest from the old man, not wanting to disturb him. Aris followed.

"You not seeming to enjoy yourself," he said.

Shianne sighed. Their language barrier was getting better, but what truly amazed her was how well he could sense her moods. She had to tell someone and she knew he would never breathe a word of this to anyone. Aris was safe.

"It's this whole thing with Erickson and the baby," she confessed. Once she started, she found the words rushing out of her all at once. "He doesn't want it and Tedi doesn't want it and it's so unfair that two people who don't want something should get it by accident. Sure, he's going to take responsibility for it, but I know my brother. Everything's about him. He'll use the baby to make himself more appealing to women and he might even love his kid, but it's always going to come second to him."

Aris tilted his head, his eyes searching her face for a moment before he spoke. "Do you want a baby?"

Shianne swallowed hard. That was the question, wasn't it? What exactly was she jealous of? "I don't know," she admitted. "I've never really thought about being a mother, even before I Settled. I grew up in a time where that's what a woman was supposed to think about, but I didn't. I don't know if it was because I thought I'd have time because vampires age so slowly or because I didn't want a kid. Then it was too late."

"You envy the choice."

Shianne nodded in agreement. "That's it, I think. Tedi could have this amazing life, so different than what she has now, better, but she doesn't want it. I don't know if I do, but I do know that I'm not happy with where my life is now."

The words came out before she'd even realized she was going to say them. That was it. She didn't necessarily want a baby. She just knew she didn't want her life how it was now.

"I want something more than...something more than what I have. Not money or fame," she clarified. "I want my life to actually mean something."

Aris reached out and wrapped one gloved hand around hers. His face was serious, his eyes almost black. He spoke in Greek so there would be no miscommunication. "Then make it mean something."

****

"Let me get this straight," Shianne said. "*Leo*, my little brother who's spent more time with books than people over the last century and a half, invited a girl to come to dinner?"

"Wait a minute," Pru said. "Let me see if I've got this. Erickson's not out flirting with girls because he got one pregnant back home and he's preparing to be a father. Alexander's not flirting with guys because he's pining over the one he can't have, and Leo isn't locking himself in the library because he's out with a girl?"

Val nodded.

Pru climbed up onto the back of the sofa and rested her elbows on her knees. "Anyone else feeling like they just pulled an Alice and went through the looking glass?"

"I think it's wonderful," Val said sternly.

"Oh, that's not what I meant," Pru hurried to explain. "I think it's great that Leo's acting like a normal person for once. I'm just a little freaked out by the fact that the boys have seemed to all done complete one-eighties."

Shianne patted Pru's shoulder. "That's what happens when people start to grow up." A strange, wistful expression came over her face. "Priorities change. People realize what they really want."

Pru gave her sister a curious look. "Are you changing?"

Shianne's eyes sparkling and a secretive smile played around her lips. "You know, maybe I am."

"Great," Pru muttered as Shianne headed off, probably to find Aris. "Everybody's changing but me."

"Pru, have you seen Dr. Darcy?" Val asked. "I think I'm getting a laugh line."

"Last I saw him, he was having a cigarette with one of the camera guys," Pru said. She pulled her phone out of her pocket. "Disgraceful if you ask me. A doctor who smokes." She looked up and saw that she was talking to herself. "Apparently not everyone is changing."

She climbed off the couch and headed for her room. She wanted to call Karson, partly because she wanted to know how he was doing, but also because she just needed to talk to someone who wasn't going all weird. She was pulling up her contacts when the door in front of her opened and she nearly walked right into Alexander.

"Oh, sorry." She stumbled back a step, expecting a joke about watching where she was going.

Nothing.

Alexander, her favorite brother, barely even looked at her as he walked across the hall to the bathroom. Pru stared. His hair was a mess and he still looked half-asleep. He was only wearing a pair of shorts – a compromise he'd reached with Heir regarding his usual sleeping attire or lack thereof – so there was nothing to prevent Pru from seeing the scratches and dried blood on her brother's neck, back and chest.

Her eyes widened and she hurried away, completely mortified. She wasn't as naïve as most people thought, and she knew her siblings had sex. Well, except for Leo. Until recently, he'd never even been interested in talking to anyone else, let alone sleeping with them. She also knew that some humans even liked things rough, so it made sense that vampires, who were so much more intense than humans, would get...like that. She'd just never seen her brother looking like he'd gotten into a cat fight. Girl or actual feline – either one would work.

By the time she reached her room, her embarrassment was starting to be replaced by concern. Like she'd said, she wasn't naïve. She'd seen Alexander have hickeys before and there had always been men coming and going at all hours in various states of undress. This was different. She assumed that there hadn't been men coming home with Alexander out of respect for their grandmother. She knew he was finding them because he was coming in at all hours and that was how Alexander dealt with life in general, but now she was starting to wonder if her brother wasn't bringing his 'dates' home because he didn't want anyone knowing what he was doing.

Pru looked down at the phone in her hand and tossed it on her bed. She couldn't call Karson. There was no way she could pretend to be okay, and hell would freeze over before she talked to her friend about her brother's sex life.

****

Alexander barely glanced in the mirror when he entered the bathroom, but when he got out of the shower, he got a good look at the scratches on his chest. He turned and saw similar furrows on his back. He shrugged. Since he'd eaten well last night, they'd be healed soon. He had to admit, he'd been surprised that the men had been able to do what they'd promised. Vampire skin wasn't easy to cut. Then again, this was Paris and the city had just as much dark dangerousness to offer as it did light and beauty.

He'd gone out as he had every night since he'd found Pierre in that little candy shop. Those few minutes he'd been with the young man, he'd been able to forget, and he craved that as much as he craved blood. And it wasn't just some fun quickie he wanted either. For the first time in his life, he was tapping into a darkness he'd never known he'd had. He didn't know if it was a part of his vampire nature or the result of having lost the one thing that had given his life meaning. All he knew was that he had found a seedier side of the city and there were plenty of men who were more than willing to let him vent his darkness.

It wasn't until he was back in his room getting dressed that he realized Pru had seen him. He glanced at the bed and saw the blood on the sheets. He'd probably been a mess when he'd nearly run into her.

He should apologize to her, he knew. Even offer some sort of off-hand explanation. But he didn't want to. He was sick of having to explain himself to everyone. He was going to live forever and it was his life. If it was going to be as bleak and empty as it looked right now, he deserved to find some way to make it tolerable, because tolerable was about all he could hope for without *him*.

CHAPTER TWENTY

Everyone was trying very hard not to stare at Saraleti, but only Di and Heir seemed to be succeeding. Even Erickson found himself watching the girl. Or, more accurately, watching Leo with the girl. It was kind of cute, he had to admit, seeing his brother so completely smitten. Alexander had always been such a confident kid, even though he'd been attracted to men during a time when that wasn't only unpopular, but dangerous. Erickson hadn't really had the opportunity to see the whole 'puppy love' kind of thing since Alexander'd had to hide it. Erickson had always worried about Leo when it came to love. Girls, boys, it didn't seem to matter. Leo had just never been interested. For a while, Erickson had thought it was because they were only around humans and Leo wasn't attracted to them as a whole, but the closer he'd watched, the more he'd realized that Leo was just so self-contained, he never allowed himself to get close to anyone.

Erickson knew if he shared his observations with anyone, even

Shianne, they'd be surprised. He'd always given off the air of caring more about himself than anyone else, but his family always came first. Granted, he was a close second, but he'd give his life for any of them without a second thought. Okay, maybe a second thought, but he'd eventually do the right thing.

Just like he was going to do with his baby.

He glanced at Shianne, but she was engaging Saraleti in a conversation about her travels with the ballet. Something was wrong with his sister, like something had broken between them and he didn't know how to fix it. And it wasn't just that he didn't know how to fix it. He didn't even know what had happened. His eyes narrowed as he saw Shianne lean over to Aris and say something that made the human laugh. Was that it, Erickson wondered. Had the human done something to turn Shianne against her brother? Or, worse yet, had Shianne turned to the human because Erickson hadn't been there for her?

Before he could think any more about what was going on with Shianne, Pru demonstrated her natural ability for creating a horrifying and uncomfortable situation with a single question.

"So, Saraleti, what we're all dying to know but everyone except me is too polite to ask is, do you have a boyfriend?"

****

"Your family is very kind," Saraleti said as she and Leo slowly walked around the small Parisian garden behind the house the Vamps had rented.

"My sister," Leo began. "Saraleti, I must apologize...her behavior...I do not know..."

She put her hand on his arm and stopped him from speaking. "It is quite all right. She is a charming child. Very – what is the English word? – precocious."

Leo nodded. He would have agreed with her about anything just to feel the touch of her hand on his arm. Even through his coat and her gloves, he imagined he could feel her hand. He had never liked to be touched or held, not since his mother, but Saraleti, he found he did not mind so much.

"I was pleased that you asked me to visit," Saraleti said. She motioned towards a bench and they moved to sit down next to each other. "I do not know many vampires and I have always wondered what it must be like, to live in a world like yours."

"Like mine?" Leo did not understand.

She gave him a smile so sad that his heart ached. He wished he could take her hands in his and tell her that all would be well, but he still feared that his actions would not be welcome.

"With such a loving family. It must be wonderful to have others with whom you can speak and share your dreams." She looked down at her hands. "To have dreams of your own."

A pang of guilt went through Leo. He had never stopped to consider himself fortunate. He had only felt bitterness at what was hidden from him. He loved his family, but he saw now that he had never truly appreciated them. He pushed the thoughts aside for future musings and focused on the girl next to him.

"You do not have dreams of your own?" he asked. "You are a beautiful dancer. Your future is bright."

"It is not my future," Saraleti said. "I love the ballet, and my dream is to dance, but I will never see it."

"Why not?" Leo found his hand reaching for her.

"Because I am not like you, or your family," Saraleti said. She looked away from him, her eyes taking on a far-off look that told him she was not seeing the garden. "I was born human, raised by a mother who neither loved nor wanted me, abandoned by a father I never knew. I will not speak of the cruelties to which she subjected me, but only say that when I was near your sister's age, she was approached by a vampire couple who were visiting our small town. She sold me to them for two days' worth of food, though I was told she asked for more."

Leo could not take his eyes off of her as she spoke. He could not imagine anyone being willing to part with this exquisite creature for all the gold in the world. How could anyone not love her?

"They were kind to me, in their way. I was well-fed, educated, cultured in the arts, music and ballet. It is thanks to them that I found dance, but I was never their daughter. I was more a living doll or a pet. As I grew older, I saw that I would never be allowed to leave. They intended to keep me as their plaything. One night, just after my eighteenth birthday, I tried to escape. Mama caught me and it was that night she Turned me into what I am."

Leo swallowed hard. Di and Val had been Turned, but he knew

that both had agreed to the change, wanted it even. That had made sense to him. Humans had always been obsessed with immortality. Vampires were always very particular about whom they chose to Turn. It was one of their greatest unspoken laws. He had never considered that someone would be Turned against their will.

"Even after I knew what I was, I tried again to escape." She glanced at him, then looked down again. "Three years it took me to build the courage. I did not get far, and this time, Mama and Papa had a way to keep me from ever trying again."

She took a deep breath and Leo could see that she was shaking. He did not believe it was from the cold and when she opened her mouth, he understood. Blood rushed in his ears as a surge of anger like nothing he had felt since his mother's death rushed through him.

Her fangs were gone, shaved down until they appeared as human teeth.

"I could not feed myself and I knew I could tell no one what I was. My choices were to stay and live, or run and die. I chose to live."

Leo took her hands between his now, his previous fears forgotten in the overwhelming protectiveness he felt towards this young woman. "You are safe here, Saraleti. Safe with us."

She looked up at him, her dark eyes swimming with tears. "I know."

****

Heir stared at his youngest son. He couldn't remember the last time he'd been so pleasantly shocked. Alexander's successful clothing line had been surprising and positive. Taylor Ann's recent bout of illness was shocking but not in a good way. Leo coming to him with this request was the last thing he would've expected and it gave him a hope for his son that he hadn't experienced in many years.

Di was equally as surprised, but she didn't seem to be feeling the same positive emotions Heir was. "You want to do what?"

Leo's eyes held a brilliant light that, despite their color, reminded Heir of Treasa. His expression, however, was impassive. "I wish to invite Saraleti to accompany us to Edinburgh for the holidays."

"What about her family?" Di asked.

Leo couldn't hide the flash of anger that crossed his eyes or how his mouth flattened. "They are not good examples of our kind."

Heir had a feeling that there was more to the story than what Leo was saying, but he also realized something else. Leo wasn't just smitten by the girl. He was in love with her. Heir recognized the look because he had seen it on his own face when he had met Treasa. Heir had loved his first wife, and he loved Val, though in a different way, but he had only truly fallen in love once. For some of their kind, it was like that. Humans called them soul-mates, but the name wasn't what mattered. Once found, there was no going back. No one could ever replace that One Love. Heir had wondered over the years if any of his children would be the same.

It was a blessing and curse, loving someone with that much of your being. Heir saw that in Leo now, and he couldn't tell his son no.

"If she will come, she is welcome," Heir said. He ignored Di's surprised look. Very rarely did he do something that she didn't expect.

Leo nodded and stood. "I will ask her. Thank you."

****

Saraleti had come to see the Vamp family every day since their first meeting. She liked it there with them, the feeling of family. She had a sense that something was not quite right in the harmony between the vampires, but it was still more of a true family than she had ever known. Her ballet company was wonderful, but there was always this secret between them. And her parents...

She shook her head. It was the last day the Vamps would be in Paris. She did not wish to spoil it by thinking of Mama and Papa. They had not been pleased with where she had been spending her time, but she knew they were too frightened of the American vampires to forbid her from going. The Vamp family was rich, famous and powerful, and much bigger than her own family of three.

"Saraleti!" Leo came out to greet her.

He took her hand as she walked up the front steps, releasing it once she had entered the house. He was always like that. So polite and careful, never making too much contact with her. She knew he cared for her. She could read it in his eyes whenever he looked at her, but he never forced his affections on her. He was younger than she physically as he had told her he had just become sixteen, but he had been born nearly a full century before she had been Turned. He often spoke as if he were still in a past time. His manners and bearing spoke of having been raised outside of the often crass and crude ways of the modern world. At times, she found herself watching him, captivated by his beauty, by the way he moved, by how totally unaware he was of his own appeal. She'd never seen anyone quite like him before.

And then there was the way he looked at her. As if she were some precious object to be cherished and protected. Men had been propositioning her since before she had been Turned, but she knew they had only wanted one thing. She had fans of her work, but they did not see the real her. Leo did. She had told him things she had never spoken of to anyone, and still he did not cast her away. Instead, he treated her with kindness, courtesy and a tenderness she had never experienced before, and yet did not ask for anything in return.

She knew her feelings for him were growing, and they frightened her, but she did not think she could stop them. Perhaps, then, she told herself, it was for the best that the Vamps were leaving. Once they were apart, Leo would forget about her. The thought pained her, but she had already accepted that this time with him would be something she would only cherish in her memory.

"I wish to ask you something," Leo said as he sat next to her.

Saraleti smiled. He looked nervous. It surprised her how well she had come to know his moods, even in this short time. "Yes?" she asked.

"As you know, we leave for Edinburgh tomorrow morning," Leo began. "It is my father's birthplace and now my grandmother shall even be accompanying us."

Saraleti was puzzled. Surely he did not just want to tell her about his grandmother traveling with the family?

"I wish for you to come with us as well."

The words came out in such a rush that she almost did not believe that she heard him correctly. Then she saw his face and knew that she had, indeed, understood what he had said.

For one wild and hopeful moment, she saw it. Leaving France behind. No longer being under the rule of Mama and Papa. Being able to pursue her dreams without fear of them being ripped away. Being with Leo and his family.

Then reality descended and she knew she could not accept his invitation. Mama and Papa would never let her leave, and if she defied them, she would never be able to return. What would become of her when Leo tired of her, for she knew he would. She was a lesser vampire, Turned and crippled by her parents for her own good. She could not feed herself, and had nothing to contribute to the talented Vamp family.

"Thank you, Leo," she said softly. "But Mama and Papa will never let me go, and I cannot go against them. I must do as they say."

She could not bear to see the hurt in Leo's eyes, not when her own heart was breaking. She stood and hurried away from the house where she had spent the only happy hours she had ever experienced when she was not dancing. She let the tears come as she fled. She would mourn now, lock away her precious memories and one day would take them out again when the joy finally outweighed the sadness.

****

Leo had not been able to sleep, so his packing was completed before the others woke. He stayed in his room as he heard the others bustling about. He sat at the edge of his bed, his luggage waiting by the door. He would not join the others until they were ready to go. He did not wish to have his father or Di ask where Saraleti was. He did not think he could bear to tell them that she had run from him.

He looked down at his hands. It was strange, he thought, how the return to a common state after a minor disruption could feel so wrong. He had never been one to become infatuated or even allow himself to care deeply about anyone, not since his mother. Even as much as he loved his family, he kept them at a distance. He had sworn to himself that he never again wished to feel the pain he had felt at his mother's death, and he had known the only way to do that was to isolate himself.

He should have known better than to allow himself to become attached to Saraleti. The pain was not as deep as it had been with his mother, but it was enough that he longed for the numbness he had perfected over the years. Perhaps, he told himself, it was better that things ended this way, before he had lost himself. He had seen what losing his mother had done to his father, and he knew if he allowed himself to care for Saraleti more than he already did, he would not survive her loss.

Someone knocked on his door. It would be Di, he knew, or perhaps one of his sisters sent on Di's behalf. They would want to know if he was ready to leave. He stood and crossed to the door. His mouth was open, the words prepared, but when he opened the door, the woman standing there was not who he had thought.

"Saraleti?" He breathed her name, afraid to blink for fear she would disappear.

She adjusted the strap of the bag that hung at her side. "If the offer still stands, I would like to come with you."

She was standing straight, her shoulders back and chin up, but Leo could see the trembling of her lips, the way her fingers were shaking. With a start, he realized that she believed he would turn her away, either angered by her original rejection or perhaps having decided that he had not truly meant the invitation. Her eyes started to fill with tears and he suddenly realized he had waited too long to answer.

"Yes!" he blurted out. If he had been human, his face would have been red. "Yes, the offer still stands. I would love nothing more than for you to come with me."

He had not intended to say 'me' but rather 'us,' but he didn't correct the slip. He meant what he had said. He wanted her to come with him. Everything he had been trying to push down and tell himself that it was better not to feel came flooding forward and he did not try to stop it. He had a feeling that he could not have stopped it if he had tried. Some things were simply meant to be.

CHAPTER TWENTY-ONE

The flight from Paris to Edinburgh was longer than Taylor Ann had anticipated, but it gave her and Stephen the opportunity to talk in relative privacy. The company jets were large and roomy, almost as nice as the one the Vamps' owned. The main difference was that on the Vamps' plane, they didn't have to remind a camera crew that conversations between Taylor Ann and her therapist were confidential. Back home, the camera crew would've just filmed a couple faraway shots to use for establishing timelines or filler, then left her alone. Ever since the tabloids had taken up their crusade for something romantic happening between vampire and therapist, however, the cameras were always on Taylor Ann when Stephen was around.

"Doesn't that bother you?" she asked, letting her hair cover the side of her face so her mouth couldn't be seen by the cameras. Pru had told her that lip-readers had been known to interpret parts of private conversations.

"What?" Stephen asked as he leaned back in the chair.

They'd chosen a space furthest away from the Vamps, but they still had to speak quietly to prevent the vampires or the microphones from picking up anything.

"Them," Taylor Ann said. "The constant attention from the cameras, the network hoping to catch something scandalous just to improve ratings."

"Do you worry about the show's ratings?" Stephen asked.

Taylor Ann scowled. "It's doing fine. Better than fine actually. Pru says there are rumors that the network's going to order two more seasons before this one's done filming." She twisted a chunk of her hair around her finger. "Pru says people are fascinated by the vampire-human relationships and that's why they keep writing stories about us, especially now that the stories about Tedi and Erickson are starting to go away."

"Does it bother you that they're writing things that aren't true, or that now they're treating you like they treat Shianne?"

Taylor Ann stared at him for a moment. How did he always do that, know what she was thinking even when she couldn't put the thoughts together herself?

"I love my sister," she began. Stephen nodded, but didn't say anything. "But I never wanted to be like her, famous for...well, for just being who she is. Until the whole Vamp Tramp spray, she'd never done anything but show up at parties and flirt with guys. I mean, she gave Dad ideas sometimes on clothes, but she never worked at anything." She looked down at her hands. "And now I'm afraid that the press is going to start acting like I'm her, like what happened before was because I wanted attention...their attention."

"And?" he prompted after she'd been silent for a few seconds.

Taylor Ann was afraid that what she was going to say next would be taken wrong, but she knew she had to say it. She just had to remind herself that she trusted Stephen, and that he would never jump to conclusions.

"And I'm afraid that this is going to be too much and you're going to leave me."

Stephen leaned forward. When he put a hand on her shoulder, Taylor Ann flinched and wanted to draw away. She could see the cameras in her mind's eye, zooming in on the touch. Only Stephen's firm grip on her shoulder kept her from moving.

"I knew what I was getting into when I agreed to be your therapist, Taylor," he said. "And I'm not going to let the media undo all of the great progress you've made these last few months."

"But what if you get in trouble?" Taylor Ann asked, looking up at Stephen. He'd been her rock, the one person she'd known she could go to with any problem, no matter how big or small. She didn't think she could do this without him.

"What are you in control of?" Stephen asked, his voice firm.

"Myself," Taylor Ann answered automatically.

"And what can't you control?"

"Everything else." She took a deep breath.

"Are you responsible for the show?"

She shook her head.

"Are you responsible for what others say about you or your family?"

She shook her head again.

"Am I your responsibility?"

Another head shake.

"Tell me."

She didn't need him to be more specific. It was the same thing they'd worked on every day since he'd first started seeing her. "I'm responsible for myself, to take care of myself. I am responsible for my own actions. I am not responsible for the actions of others. I cannot control everything. I have to see myself clearly and love myself. Those who love me will love me no matter what, and those who don't aren't my problem."

"Very good." Stephen smiled at her. "I am so proud of how far you've come, Taylor."

"It doesn't feel like it's very far," she admitted.

"Did you eat today?" he asked.

She gave him a puzzled look. "You know I did. You were there with the rest of the family."

"You've been stressing about this whole tabloid thing every time we go out, but you haven't started skipping meals again."

She hadn't realized it until Stephen pointed it out. He was right. She hadn't missed a single meal or balked at taking what she needed.

"That's progress," he said. "You're going to have issues you need to talk out, and you're going to have difficult times, but that's what I'm here for." He reached out and squeezed her hand, and this time she didn't try to pull away. "But the fact that you were able to resist returning to those destructive behaviors we talked about, and do it without needing me to remind you, says that you're much stronger than you think."

Taylor Ann smiled and felt a weight lift off of her chest. She really was getting better, and that's what she really wanted. To be whole again. She glanced back at the rest of her family and some of her joy faded. She wanted them all to be whole again, but something told her that things were just going to get worse from here.

****

Saraleti had never imagined Scotland would be so beautiful. She and her parents had traveled around France but they had always returned to Paris. In a century, she had never been outside of her country. The plane had frightened her, but Leo had spoken to her in a soft voice, telling her stories of the places he had been. In each one, she could hear him imply that should she but speak it, he would take her to these places, show her the world. The feelings she had been trying to deny were close to the surface now and she did not know what to do.

She remained silent as the Vamp family and the men filming them traveled from the airport to a beautiful house. She heard Di mention that it had been built in the early eighteen hundreds, but Saraleti could not understand why the elder vampire sounded so upset at this. Truly the home was magnificent. There were rooms for each of them and her parents' entire house would have fit in the main living space.

The Vamp family had seemed surprised to see her coming with them, but none had asked her why or how it had come to be. She appreciated that. She did not wish to share her reasons. Perhaps with Leo, in private, but she did not yet feel comfortable enough with the others, though they had been nothing but kind to her. The two other young men in the family appeared to be preoccupied with other matters, but even they had greeted her politely.

Left alone to unpack, she found herself restless once her meager possessions had been put away. She did not want to be seen as snooping, so she remained in her room, admiring the beautiful stonework. The moon shone through her window, drawing her attention and as she opened them, she saw that they lead onto a balcony.

A movement caught the corner of her eye and she gasped.

"Saraleti." A familiar voice kept her from crying out.

"Leo, I am sorry. You startled me."

"I apologize." He stepped forward. The moonlight threw shadows across his face and Saraleti thought that she could glimpse the handsome man he would become. "The balcony runs along the entire second floor." He gestured behind him.

She nodded, her racing heart calming.

"Would you like to sit?" he asked, motioning to a pair of antique wooden chairs that sat between the two windows.

She nodded again, giving him a shy smile that made his face light up. It would never cease amazing her that a look from her could make someone like Leo Vamp so happy.

****

Leo had chosen the room next to Saraleti's before any of his siblings had even made it up the stairs. He saw their looks of surprise – he usually waited until they chosen and took what was left as he generally had no preference – but had not explained his actions. If the twinkle in his little sister's eyes had been any indication, he had not needed to explain, at least to her. He had unpacked quickly and then had gone to stand on the balcony. He had been able to hear well enough into Saraleti's room to know if she walked back into the house so he might follow. He did not know how long she would choose to stay with them and he wished to savor every moment. When she had stepped out onto the balcony, he had to catch his breath. The moonlight had made her skin translucent, and her hair nearly as dark as his. His heart had thudded painfully against his ribs and he had wondered once again at the enormity of what he felt.

Now, they were sitting side-by-side, barely an inch between them and he felt as if the air was full of electricity, sparking between the two of them. He did not know if she felt it too, but he never wanted this night to end.

"This is your family's home?" she asked.

"No." He shook his head. He felt shy even though they had

spoken many times over the past week. She had shared something personal with him, and now he wished to share something with her. "My grandmother, Rupa, was part of a gypsy tribe that passed through Scotland in the thirteen hundreds. She fell in love with Alban, the only child of prominent, wealthy landowners. They married and my father was born at some point during the middle of the century. They do not know exactly when. They were happy for a long time, but in fifteen seventy-two, my grandfather was murdered. None of us children know the details as my father will never speak of it, and we would never ask my grandmother to recall such a horrible time."

He paused, stealing a glance to see if Saraleti was listening. She was, a look of such compassion on her face that the last of his shyness melted away.

"My grandmother, Di and my father fled to Greece. Those who murdered my grandfather burnt his land, then divided it among humans." He pointed to an area of shops and apartments to the east. "Those stand where my family home once did."

"It must be difficult," Saraleti said. "For your grandmother to return."

Leo nodded thoughtfully. "This is the first time she has come back. She and my father. I believe she came to support him."

"You have such a kind family," Saraleti said. She looked up at the moon. "You have had tragedy, but have not let it define you."

Leo felt a twinge of guilt as he thought of the years he had spent searching for answers. That, he told himself, was different. Once he knew the truth, he could move on.

"Though you fight, you are always here for each other."

He could hear the wistful note in her voice.

"You are truly blessed to have a place where you know you belong."

"I do not always feel that way," Leo surprised himself by the admission. "I am...different than my siblings."

Saraleti gave him a look of puzzlement.

He continued, wanting her to understand, "They enjoy the world, adapt to the changes. I do not. I stay the same. I know they love me and I love them, but they do not understand me, nor I them." He smiled a slightly sad smile. "I believe sometimes they think something is wrong with me."

Saraleti reached over and Leo held his breath, thinking that she would rest her hand on his arm for a moment and the night would become one of his most cherished memories. Instead, she slipped her hand into his, threading her fingers between his. He swallowed hard, unable to look away from where her fingers were laced with his. A sweet aching longing filled him and he knew now, without a doubt, that he was in love with her. He had never imagined he could feel this way about anyone, but he knew that from this moment, he was changed and would never be the same again. This, he was certain, had been the way his father had felt about his mother and his fingers tightened around hers at the thought of losing her.

"Leo?" Her voice was timid, as if she was unsure she had done the right thing.

He looked up at her and smiled. A look of relief washed over her face and she relaxed back in the chair. For a moment, he was afraid she would take her hand away, but she did not. They sat in silence for hours, watching the moon and the stars, their hands linked until, finally, Leo knew they must return to their rooms. Only after they moved towards their separate rooms did their hands finally part, and Leo felt the loss so deeply than he almost turned and asked her to come with him, just to lie next to each other with hands clasped, but he resisted. He would do nothing that would damage her reputation or cause her to think he would treat her with disrespect. Instead, he smiled at her and waited for her to safely return to her room before he too, went inside.

Sleep came surprisingly quickly, bringing with it dreams of dark marks and burned flesh. When he woke with a start, he was breathing hard as if he had been running. It took him longer to fall back asleep as he dreaded the return of a nightmare he could not remember, but he focused on the feeling of Saraleti's hand in his and, this time, he slept soundly.

CHAPTER TWENTY-TWO

Erickson really didn't want to take a tour around Edinburgh. In fact, all he really wanted to do was go home. This trip was supposed to have been an opportunity for the Vamp family to go international. He and Shianne should've been out at all of the hottest clubs going home with the best-looking men and women in every country they visited.

Instead, he was watching his sister fawn over a human. And not just any human. Their grandmother's feeder, for crying out loud. This preoccupation meant she didn't have time for Erickson. Of course, there had been times in their history when Shianne hadn't been available to go out – usually due to something planned with Val – but by then he'd at least had Alexander as back-up. The younger Vamp was just as good at divide and conquer as their sister, even if most of the men involved generally considered themselves straight.

Problem was, Alexander wasn't in any better a mood than

Erickson. In fact, Erickson was pretty sure the only difference between the crap time they were both having was that Alexander was at least getting laid. He hadn't seen any of his younger brother's conquests wandering around, but Erickson had seen enough hickeys on his brother's neck to feel it was a safe assumption.

"Allow me."

Erickson looked over at where his youngest brother was holding up an umbrella to shield he and the ballerina from the few rays of sun that escaped Scotland's heavy winter cloud cover.

Then there was Leo. Erickson frowned. It wasn't that he begrudged his littlest brother getting the girl for the first time. He just wasn't used to being around a woman – or pretty much anyone attracted to men – who didn't so much as give him a second glance. It wasn't that he wanted Saraleti. Well, he might've if Leo hadn't liked her. She was cute. But, as much as Erickson knew he could be a jerk at times, he'd never do anything like that to his brother. It just sucked, not being the one everyone was looking at.

"Do you remember, Di, the fields that used to be here?" Rupa's voice came from in front of Erickson, pulling him from his thoughts about himself. "We would gather flowers for the dinner table."

He hadn't realized until now how sad his grandmother and Di had been as they'd walked through the streets. His father, however, was nearly impossible to read. Erickson looked over at Di, the woman who had been as much responsible for raising him as his mother and step-mothers had been. She had always been the constant. Even after Treasa had died and his father had gone into mourning, Di had been there. For the first time in his life, Erickson realized that Di had once had a life that hadn't involved watching out for the Vamp kids.

"My farm was over there," Di said softly.

"You had a farm?" Pru sounded as surprised as Erickson felt.

"I did," Di said. She gave Pru a smile. "We raised sheep." The smile lost some of its sadness. "I was a human for more than fifty years before I began watching Vamp children." She glanced at Heir, perhaps remembering him as a child.

It was strange, Erickson thought, to remember that Di was actually older than his father, that Rupa had Turned her to be Heir's nanny. He had memories of his father before Heir had Settled, but vampires aged so slowly that Heir had always seemed to be the same age as Di, even before he'd Settled.

"Oh! Was the castle there too!" Pru asked excitedly. "Did you know the people who lived in it?"

His sister's enthusiasm was catching and Erickson found himself wanting to smile. He didn't really feel any better, and he was still completely conflicted about the whole baby thing, but he had a feeling that if he wanted to, he could make himself be in a better mood. He just wasn't sure he wanted to.

*****

Edinburgh was everything Pru had dreamed and more. The

house where they were staying had been decorated for Christmas by some people the network had hired, so the moment they'd stepped inside, everything was green and red and lights and evergreen. They'd spent the last two days touring the city and she'd gotten to hear stories about her father and grandmother, and even Di, growing up. They'd told her about what it had looked like back then and how her grandfather's family had been. It was strange, Pru thought, how she didn't have any actual memories of Val as a human, but she'd never had a problem remembering that Val had been Turned. It was different with Di though. Pru couldn't imagine Di as a human.

Pru knew she should be heading up to her bedroom and she was tired enough that she was thinking it might be a good idea, but she heard something that made her forget about how tired she was. Someone else was up and they'd just gone out the front door. She gave a quick glance around to see where the cameraman was and saw that he had his back to her. She took advantage of his momentary lapse in attention and hurried towards the door. When she wanted to, she could be as light on her feet as a cat, and this was one of the times she wanted to be.

She stepped out into the street in time to see blond hair and a slight build turn the corner. Alexander. She didn't even stop to think if it was a good idea. She just followed. Her brother had been so distant since the incident with Noah and he wouldn't talk to her. She'd tried, but he'd just give her a condescending smile and some excuse. She felt a stab of guilt that she hadn't pushed him harder, made him realize that even though she was having fun, she still cared.

She fully intended to talk to him, but something about the way he was walking made her think that if she spoke to him now, he would blow her off and tell her to go home. And she couldn't deny that a part of her was curious about what he was doing. If Alexander was going to a club, the cameras should be following him, but the only one following him now was her. She stayed to the shadows, a knot growing in the pit of her stomach the further they went.

Just before they reached a stretch of local businesses, Alexander turned down an alley. Pru didn't follow at first. She flattened herself against the building and strained her ears, listening for a door to shut, signaling Alexander had gone somewhere. Instead, she heard voices with thick Scottish brogues saying things she never wanted to hear, especially when she realized who they were talking about.

"He is a pretty one."

"Make him get on his knees."

"The clothes first. I want to see if vampire skin is as tough as they say."

She heard a pained cry and fury broke her free of her hiding place. She flew around the corner, throwing herself into the first human she saw. He was twice her size, but she was a vampire and she'd caught him off guard. He stumbled backwards, knocking into the other two men who'd been speaking. She heard herself screaming as she clawed at the men, and then there were hands around her arms, pulling her away, shoving her back towards the mouth of the alley.

"What the hell, Pru?!"

The haze that had clouded her vision cleared and she saw that Alexander was standing in front of her, no shirt, the top button of his pants undone, and his eyes blazing with anger. She took a step back when she realized the anger was directed at her.

"I-I thought they..." She stared at her brother's chest. She'd seen him in Paris with what she'd thought were scratch marks, now there were other marks there and she didn't know what could do that to a vampire's skin. "They were hurting you."

The sneer on Alexander's face was full of loathing and condescension. "They weren't doing anything I didn't want them to do. I'm a vampire, Pru. Don't you think I could've stopped them if I wanted to?"

Her mind was reeling but she forced herself to latch on to the one thing she knew. This wasn't normal. Sure, Alexander had always liked to party, but it had never been like this. He'd never wanted people to hurt him.

"Why are you doing this?" she asked. "Is it because of Noah?"

"You think I care about one little human?" Alexander laughed. "Come on, Pru. Don't be stupid."

Pru's temper flared and it helped clear her mind. "You're out here in an alley asking three men to hurt you and do who knows what else to you, and I'm the one who's being stupid? You've been acting like an ass ever since London and I know you're hurting, but whatever you're doing isn't the answer."

"Thanks for the psychology, little sister," Alexander said. "But if I wanted the opinion of a twelve year-old, I would've asked for it."

Tears of anger pricked at Pru's eyes. "I may be twelve, but at least I'm not acting like a spoiled child throwing a temper tantrum when he doesn't get his way. Grow up!"

Alexander took a step towards Pru, his face twisted into something almost unrecognizable. "That's funny, coming from you. That's all you want, isn't it? To grow up? Do you even know what it means to grow up? No, you don't. You think that people are actually going to listen to you, take you seriously, just because you're older? You think you're going to find love and live happily ever after? None of that's real. That's just some fairytale children, like you, tell themselves so they don't have to face the cold, hard truth that life sucks." He gave her a disgusted look. "I would tell you to grow up, but we all know that's the only thing you care about anyway."

She stared at him for a full ten seconds, then turned and ran, managing to hold back the tears until she rounded the corner and he couldn't see that he'd made her cry. She wouldn't give him that satisfaction.

CHAPTER TWENTY-THREE

Shianne had a feeling she should be paying more attention to what was going on with the rest of her family as they all prepared for Christmas Eve, but she was having a hard time thinking about anything but the fact that she'd decided to confess to Aris how she felt. She hadn't yet decided how or when, only that she wanted him to know. Her stomach was in knots as she finished wrapping her Christmas presents and seeing Aris helping Rupa put gifts under the tree didn't help anything. Shianne also knew she'd also have to talk to her grandmother if Aris returned her affections. It was a little creepy to think about wanting to make out with the guy who spent a couple days a week with her grandmother's mouth on his neck. Shianne knew there'd never been anything else between Aris and Rupa, but it would still be weird to feel like she was sharing with her grandmother.

"Your father tells me that your Christmas Eve traditions are to dress in pajamas, sit in front of the fire and tell Christmas stories?"

Rupa smiled at Shianne.

She nodded. "And we play games. Then we each choose one present to open before we go to bed." She smiled. "We started it when Dad married Treasa. She used to get so impatient, she wanted to open all of the presents on Christmas Eve, and of course Erickson and I weren't going to argue with that. Allowing us each one was their compromise."

"She was a good woman," Rupa said. "As is Val, but I do miss Treasa."

"We all do," Shianne's smile faltered.

"Well, I must go speak with Heir about the stories we will be telling tonight. I wish to tell one from my people."

"That would be wonderful, Grandmother," Shianne said. She watched Rupa leave, one camera following. The other stayed behind, but aside from the cameraman, Shianne and Aris were alone.

"Would you go into the garden with me?" Aris asked as he stood. Shianne saw him slip a thin package into his pants pocket.

She nodded, butterflies exploding in her stomach. It was time. She knew the cameras would catch it, no matter where they went, so she ignored them as she followed Aris outside. She did wish, though, that this moment would be private. It was funny, she thought, how she'd always flaunted her relationships for the cameras, and now that the cameras were on twenty-four seven, she wanted to keep this to herself. Not that she was ashamed of how she felt, but rather because she knew how rough going public would be.

She rolled her eyes at her own thoughts. Here she was, talking like everything was already set when she didn't even know for sure if he liked her like that.

Aris stopped by a bench and looked down at Shianne. He had an almost shy look on his handsome face. He took a package from his pocket and held it out to her. "I wanted to give this to you in private." He spoke in Greek as he glanced back at the cameraman. When the show aired, they would most likely have the words translated on the screen, but at least for the moment, it gave some semblance of privacy.

"Thank you," Shianne replied in Greek. Her heart was beating almost as fast as a human's as she accepted the gift. Her fingers trembled as she carefully unwrapped it. She hoped that Aris's desire to give her this in private meant that he felt the same way about her that she did about him.

The paper fell away to reveal a thin black velvet box. She opened it and there, nestled on more black velvet, was the most exquisite sapphire necklace she'd ever seen. And it looked old. Older than she was, even.

"Do you like it?" he asked nervously.

"I love it. It's beautiful." She looked up at Aris. "This must have cost you a lot. I know Grandmother pays you well..."

He smiled, relief showing on his face. "It belonged to my mother, and her mother before her. I had no sisters, so it was given to me."

Shianne swallowed hard. She'd never had someone give her something that meant anything before. Men bought her gifts, but it was always about how much something was worth, an amount they could calculate.

"May I?" He gestured to the necklace and Shianne nodded, not trusting herself to speak. He lifted the necklace from its box and stepped around behind Shianne.

Her heart stuttered as he brushed the hair away from her neck so he could fasten the clasp. All of the words she'd thought about saying were caught in her throat.

"As for how well your grandmother pays me." Aris's voice was low in her ear. "I am saving that now as I no longer have an income. I have asked her to release me as her feeder."

Shianne turned around, letting her surprise show on her face.

"I..." He paused, as if unsure how to proceed. "If I am to feed any vampire, I want it to be you."

Shianne reached up and brushed some hair back from his face. "Do you want to be my feeder, or something...else?" She knew there were humans who enjoyed feeding vampires; it was almost like a drug to some of them.

Aris gave her a tentative smile. "Something else." A shadow passed over his face. "Unless you only want..."

She stopped his words with a kiss. It was brief and almost chaste, but it told him all the things she hadn't been able to find the words to say. He slid his arms around her waist and she leaned her head against his chest, listening to the sound of his heart beating, and enjoying his warmth. For the first time in a long time, she actually felt content.

****

Pru had decided the night before that she wasn't going to let Alexander ruin her Christmas. She had vented her anger and hurt when she'd gotten home that night and then she'd told herself that if her brother wanted to act like a jerk, that was his choice. She was going to enjoy the beautifully decorated house and the time with the rest of the family. Erickson was still being moody, but the melancholy that had been hanging over Rupa, Di and Heir had faded away as the preparations for Christmas Eve had approached.

When Pru woke up at dawn on Christmas Day, she started towards Alexander's room without even thinking about it, pausing only as she reached for the doorknob. Every Christmas for as long as she could remember, she'd get up first, wake Alexander and the two of them would then wake up everyone else by blaring Christmas music. Those first few minutes when it was just the two of them, laughing and selecting what song they wanted to play, they were some of her fondest holiday memories.

She could feel tears wanting to come, but she refused to give in. Instead, she considered her options. She could do it herself, but that would just depress her. No, she decided. She needed a new partner in crime. Shianne was in such a good mood because she and Aris were now obviously together, that she might be game, but Pru wasn't sure how fast things were moving between her sister and the human, and the last thing she wanted to see right now was the two of them in bed together. Taylor Ann was really doing well thanks to Stephen, and there was no truth to the rumors about the two of them, but Pru wasn't sure if her older sister would think the tradition was too juvenile for her. Then there was Leo. He was acting much more like a normal person since Saraleti had arrived, but Pru didn't want to wake him up and have him give her that blank look that said he didn't understand what was going on.

Her shoulders slumped and she was almost ready to give up when she heard a noise from behind the door next to Leo's room. A moment later, the door opened and Saraleti appeared. Pru raised an eyebrow. She hadn't had much of a chance to talk to the ballerina since Leo pretty much monopolized the girl's time, but there was something about Saraleti that made Pru think of a glass ballerina figurine she'd had thirty or forty years ago. It had been so fragile, so delicate, that Di had insisted she keep it locked away. Pru, of course, hadn't listened, and the ballerina had broke. Saraleti looked like that, like she needed to be protected.

"I am sorry," Saraleti said in her perfect, but lightly accented English. "I did not realize anyone else was awake."

Pru put her finger over her lips and gestured for Saraleti to follow her. By the time they reached the first floor, Pru was grinning. This was perfect. She'd get Leo's girl to do the Christmas music with her and it wouldn't feel like she was replacing Alexander, and it would be her chance to make the serious ballerina smile.

"Every Christmas," Pru explained in a hushed voice. "My brother and I wake everyone up by playing music. This year, I was thinking I'd have to do it myself because Alexander – well, let's just say I don't think he's interested in Christmas traditions – but, anyway, then there you were."

Saraleti's eyes widened. "You wish for me to join your family tradition?"

Pru's smile got bigger. "Yeah. I think it'd be great." Suddenly, she realized that there was one thing she hadn't taken into consideration. She didn't know Saraleti that well. The vampire was older than Pru and Leo. She was actually closer to Alexander's age, and for all Pru knew, Saraleti would think the idea was stupid. Childish. "You don't have to if you don't want to," Pru said quickly.

"I would love to." Saraleti gave Pru a soft smile. "I was rising early in hopes of finding something I could do for your family. You have all been so kind to me, welcoming me into your home, and I have no money for gifts."

Pru waved a dismissive hand. "We don't care about things. Gifts from the heart are better." Her expression grew serious and she knew she had to tell Saraleti what the entire family felt but hadn't said. "Besides, you've already given us a great gift. Leo's always been...distant." She hesitated, then added, "He never got over our mom dying, and he just basically locks himself away. Even when he's here, he's not here, you understand? But with you around, it's almost like having my brother back. I think you saved him."

Saraleti reached out and took Pru's hands. Her eyes were shining with tears. "No, Prussia. He saved me. He and your family."

Pru didn't know what to say to that. Grown-ups didn't really talk to her like this. Well, except Alexander, but he didn't count anymore. Pru shifted uncomfortably and did one of her favorite fallbacks for when things got too emotional. She changed the subject.

"What do you say you help me get the family out of bed and downstairs so we can get Christmas started?"

Saraleti beamed and wiped her eyes. "I would like that very much."

As the pair walked into the living room, Pru thought of how nice it would be if Saraleti stayed around for a long time. It would almost be like having a sister close to her age. Not that she didn't love Taylor Ann and Shianne, but it'd be nice to have someone who wasn't trying to mother her. Leo had picked a real winner.

CHAPTER TWENTY-FOUR

At first, Alexander thought Pru had decided to ring in the New Year like she did Christmas and she'd chosen a piss-poor time to do it. They'd all been up late celebrating, and they'd still been in bed before Alexander had come home. When he'd fallen into bed, the clock had said it was four am. Now it said it was five.

He opened his mouth to yell at his sister when his brain finally registered what he'd been smelling.

Smoke.

He bolted upright, all anger gone. Now he could hear his father shouting their names. He ran out into the hallway, not bothering to put his shoes on. He was still wearing what he'd gone out in, but as he emerged into the smoke-filled corridor, he could see that the others were in their pajamas.

"Alexander!" Heir yelled from the central staircase, then coughed as he inhaled smoke. "Pru!"

A thrill of fear ran along Alexander's spine. He turned towards his sister's door. It was closed. He tried the doorknob but it was locked. He cursed. Stupid little sister worried about her privacy. He could feel the heat coming from the end of the hallway and knew he couldn't wait to try to wake her up. If she hadn't heard the sirens, she must have her headphones in.

He saw Erickson taking a step towards him and waved him off. His brother nodded once and returned to helping Val down the stairs. Alexander braced himself, then slammed into the door as hard as he could. It creaked, cracked, but didn't give.

"Leo, get Taylor Ann out of here!" Heir shouted.

Alexander hit the door again, and this time it gave. As he burst into the room, he saw Pru sitting upright, eyes wide, headphones still in.

"Alexander! What the...?!" She started to yell, then either smelled or saw the smoke.

He didn't wait for her to react. There wasn't time. He grabbed and threw her over his shoulder, ignoring her yelp of surprise and subsequent demands to be put down. He ran for the stairs, watching his father's back through a thick haze of smoke. He could barely breathe and his eyes were watering, but he trusted his instincts to take him where he needed to go.

They burst from the house and he hurried across the street to join the others. Only then did he put Pru down. She glared up at him, tears from smoke irritation leaving tracks on her dirty face. Suddenly, the memory of several nights ago came forward and he saw her face when he yelled at her, the hurt and betrayal.

He went down on his knees and threw his arms around her, all of the emotions he'd been trying to push down exploding over him at once.

"I'm sorry, Pru. I'm so sorry." He felt her arms go around him and she stroked his hair. For a moment, he could almost feel his mother's hand soothing him.

"I forgive you," Pru said softly. "It's okay. It's going to be okay."

****

Leo went to Saraleti's room first, but her door was open and she was not there. He had to find her. Something very close to panic was threatening to take over as he saw the flames licking across the walls at both ends of the corridor. He heard Alexander trying to break down Pru's door, and then his father was shouting for him to help Taylor Ann. As much as every fiber of his being protested not searching for Saraleti, he went to his sister.

She was leaning against the wall, her still thin body shaking as she coughed. He put his arm around her and started for the stairs.

"Saraleti," he said to his father.

Heir nodded and Leo felt some of the tension leave him. Surely his father had seen Saraleti escape. Leo helped Taylor Ann down the stairs and out into the cold early morning air. As he set her down, he looked around, knowing Saraleti would be distraught by what was happening. Firetrucks pulled up, sirens blaring, but he barely registered them. He was too busy trying to find her. He saw the staff and the camera crews. Val's doctor was leaning against a fence, coughing. But he did not see Saraleti.

"Stephen?" Taylor Ann's shaking voice came from behind Leo, but he did not look at her.

An icy hand gripped his heart. He grabbed his father's arm as Heir passed. "You saw Saraleti?"

Heir shook his head. "I waited for Alexander and Pru, but I did not see Saraleti. If her room was empty, she must have come down before."

"I do not see her." Leo could hear the panic in his voice. He turned towards the house and took two steps, fully intending to plunge back into the inferno.

Arms wrapped around him and Leo struggled against them. He watched firefighters run into the blaze and then, out of the corner of his eye, he saw a larger figure. Russell Beck, the head of their New York security team, ran towards the house. Vaguely, Leo was aware of Taylor Ann calling for Stephen, and he heard himself yelling Saraleti's name, but nothing seemed real.

"They'll find her, Son."

It was not until Heir spoke that Leo realized who was holding him back.

Leo drew a gasping breath as two figures appeared in the doorway, but the sound became a cry of frustration when he saw that the firefighter was assisting Stephen down the steps. Taylor Ann ran forward, throwing her arms around the human. They were both crying as a paramedic tried to pry them apart.

Then, another figure came through the smoke and Leo felt his father's arms fall away. Russell pushed past the firefighters as he carried Saraleti's limp body to the paramedics. Leo ran forward, ignoring the medics who were now trying to assess the damage to the Vamps. He fell to his knees next to Saraleti as a human female began her examination.

Beneath the mask of black soot, Saraleti's skin was paler than normal. Her eyes were closed, her expression peaceful, and still Leo searched for signs of life. His head told him that it was too late, but he refused to accept it. He took up her hand, and when the medic did not stop him, the tears began to fall. Her skin was cold despite the fire and her fingers did not curl around his.

"I'm sorry." A woman's soft voice said words he didn't want to hear. "She's gone."

His world fell away, leaving nothing but vast, bleak emptiness.

CHAPTER TWENTY-FIVE

Heir took only moments to confirm that the rest of his family was safe before he went to his son. He heard the female paramedic's pronouncement and his heart broke. He watched her move to cover Saraleti's face and Leo snarled at her, his fangs flashing and she jumped back. He quickly knelt across from his son.

"Leave us," he said to the woman. She hurried away, not needing to be told twice. He started to reach towards Leo, then stopped. The pain in the boy's eyes was familiar and, even after all these years, still near the surface. "Leo," he said softly.

The boy shook his head. His eyes were dry now, but Heir could see the streaks from where tears had first fallen. Leo had moved from the initial grief to shock. In mourning, he was very much his father's son. Heir did reach out this time and put his hand on Leo's shoulder.

"I'm so sorry."

Leo shook his head again. "She is not gone. She cannot be gone." His voice was firm.

Heir glanced over at the rest of his family. They were watching and he knew they wanted to come to Leo, but he shook his head, signaling for them to wait. He knew the only words that could break through the denial and he could not risk the others hearing, in part because what he was going to say was painful, but also because he was violating several oaths by saying it.

"When your mother died," Heir began. Leo's muscles tensed under his father's hand. "I felt the same way, that she couldn't be gone. Someone who was so full of life and love, who had so much time left, she couldn't just be gone. But she was."

"She chose to go. You said she chose to leave us. Saraleti did not want to go." Leo's voice broke. "She wanted to stay. With me."

Heir knew it was time for the truth. "Your mother didn't want to go. She was taken from us."

Leo stopped breathing for a moment, his head slowly coming up. His eyes blazed and Heir was strongly reminded of how Treasa looked when she was angry.

"You lied." The statement was flat.

Heir nodded. "I lied. I lied because your mother was killed by the *Nicolaj*, a group of vampires who use the cover of the Christian Church and the Knights Templar to obtain power and wealth."

"Why?" Leo asked. "Why did they do it? Why did you lie to us? To me?"

Heir shook his head. "I know you have questions, and I promise you that I will answer them, but now isn't the time." He looked down and Leo followed his gaze. "Now is the time to mourn."

Leo's entire body shuddered, but he didn't cry. He smoothed down Saraleti's hair. "She would not want to be returned to Paris. The vampires who raised her were cruel. She was happy here with us."

The Vamp family mausoleum still stood in the Edinburgh cemetery. "She will have a place next to my father," Heir said. He longed to wrap his arms around his son as he had when the boy was small, but he knew an embrace wouldn't be welcomed.

"No cameras," Leo said softly. "She deserves to be laid to rest with dignity and peace. She is not fodder for human entertainment."

"No cameras," Heir agreed. He didn't care what he had to promise or threaten the network with. He would make sure the funeral was private. He owed Leo that much.

He waited for his son to add more, but Leo didn't. He just sat there, one hand holding on to Saraleti's, the other stroking her hair. Even when the house began to fall in on itself, he didn't look up. It was as if there was nothing in the world but he and his lost love, and Heir knew he couldn't do anything to ease his son's pain.

CHAPTER TWENTY-SIX

Their return home to Beverly Hills should've been a blast, Shianne thought as the Vamp family exited the plane. The press was pushing the edges of the police barricade, shouting questions about the fire, about the rumors that someone had died. She winced as she heard the callous way they directed their questions, and she looked at her brother. Leo's face was as blank as it had been since the moment they'd taken Saraleti's body away.

Shianne leaned against Aris and his arm tightened around her. She didn't care that the press were having a field day with her new relationship. She was just glad to have him with her. He and Rupa had announced that they would return to the United States with the family for continued support during this time, though Shianne did wonder how much of it was because of the fire and how much was Erickson's baby. It would be, after all, Rupa's first great-grandchild.

The Vamp family was silent as Ricardo drove them home. No

one said it, but Shianne knew they were all glad to be back. She still didn't know if the network had canceled their last two weeks in Scotland or if Heir had done it, though she suspected the latter. She remembered how her father had been after Treasa had died, and Leo was reminding her very much of Heir right now. The thing was, Heir'd had his children to help pull him back. Leo had family, but he wouldn't reach out to them.

When they reached the house, Shianne showed her grandmother and Aris to the guest rooms across the hall from her bedroom.

"May I talk with you for a moment?" Rupa asked before Shianne could leave.

All Shianne wanted to do at the moment was sleep, but she forced a smile and nodded. "Of course."

Rupa sat on the edge of the bed and patted the space next to her. Aris stood awkwardly in the doorway for a moment before excusing himself to unpack. The transition was still taking some getting used to.

"I am pleased that Aris makes you happy," Rupa began. "But I must ask if you have discussed what he's going to do when it's time for me to return to Greece."

"I thought he wasn't your feeder anymore?" Shianne asked, confused. She'd seen her grandmother sharing the other feeders and there hadn't been any new bite marks on Aris's neck. They hadn't crossed that line yet.

"He's not," Rupa said. "But his life is in Greece." She gestured around her. "Or do you expect him to make a new one here in

Beverly Hills?" She gave her grand-daughter a soft smile. "He is human, after all. We can spend decades in the same place because we know we have centuries more to explore the world. Human lives are fleeting."

"I know," Shianne said. "And we haven't talked about it. Between the fire and the funeral...the timing just wasn't right."

"I have a suggestion." Rupa sounded hesitant. "I have noticed that you don't seem to be quite as content with your life in the spotlight as you once were."

Shianne gave her a startled look. She'd thought she'd been hiding it well.

"When things have settled down here and I return to Greece, instead of asking Aris to choose between you and his home, why don't you come with us?"

Shianne stared at her grandmother for nearly a full minute, her mind racing. Leave America? Leave her family? Her grandmother was right that time moved differently for vampires than it did for humans, but the thought of leaving for an open-ended amount of time was frightening. But, she had to admit that it also had its appeal. No cameras following her around. She and Aris could live in a little bubble in Greece, spending their days in the garden, walking the beaches, swimming. She and her grandmother could spend time together too, get to know each other as adults.

Finally, she nodded. "All right. I'll do it. Once things quiet down a bit, I'll talk to my father and make sure there aren't any contractual issues with me leaving."

As her grandmother hugged her, Shianne felt as if a weight had been lifted from her shoulders. She hadn't realized how much pressure all of the attention had put on her. Now that there was an end in sight, the relief was nearly overwhelming.

****

Heir's phone began to ring even as he stepped into the house. A quick look at the screen told him that it was the new network president. He sighed, but answered the call, heading for his office for some privacy.

"Now, I know you're probably busy and jet-lagged, so I'll make the business quick," Wendy McMillan said. "I've sent you a video of some footage one of our men shot the night of the fire. He'd been outside shooting some B-roll when he caught something...questionable. Of course, he didn't know it was suspicious until the fire started."

Hiram pulled up his email and opened the attachment. He might not have been fond of all of this technology, but he made sure he knew how to work it. He watched it through once, then sat down and watched it again.

Two figures in dark, hooded outfits were running away from the house. It was impossible to tell if they were male or female, or what they looked like, but the one thing Heir was almost certain of was that they weren't human. They hadn't done anything blatant, but there was something about the smoothness of their movements that told him they were vampire.

"I'm going to have to turn this over to the police, Heir," Wendy said. "But I wanted you to see it first so you could tell your family. I know your son lost a friend and I didn't want him to find out when the police came to talk to the family."

"Why would they need to speak with my family?" Heir paused the video.

"The fire wasn't an accident," Wendy said. "So investigators are going to question everyone who was at the house that night. That includes your family."

"Thank you for the notice, Wendy," he said absently. "Please keep me informed of the situation."

He hung up before she finished agreeing. His mind was already figuring out his next move. First, he needed to tell Di. She would understand the far-reaching impact of the video. Then, he would need to tell the rest of the family that the fire was going to be ruled suspicious and that the police would be speaking with them. The only thing he hadn't yet decided was if he was going to risk telling them the whole truth, including what he'd shared with Leo the night of the fire. If he did, he knew it would change everything.

CHAPTER TWENTY-SEVEN

Taylor Ann was curious about her father calling a family meeting so soon after they'd arrived home, but she reminded herself of what Stephen said, that worry wouldn't do any good and that no matter what happened, she could get through it. She lifted her chin as she joined the others in her father's office, determined to show everyone that she could be strong on her own. Still, she couldn't help but wish that Stephen was still here. She'd gotten so used to him being around all the time that not having him at her side felt strange.

Everyone was unusually quiet as they found places to sit, their attention focused on Heir so they didn't have to look at each other. Meetings in Heir's office meant that he didn't want the cameras around and that usually meant either a discussion about vampirism that humans didn't need to know about or something bad had happened. Based on the events of the past few months, she was guessing the latter.

"There is no way for me to ease into this," Heir said. "One of the camera crew caught two people running away from the house the night of the fire. They're ruling it suspicious."

While her siblings stared at their father, looking shocked, Taylor Ann immediately scanned the room for Leo, concerned about how he would take this news.

"The police will be coming to speak with everyone who was there that night, and I expect you all to give them your full cooperation."

Taylor Ann's stomach dropped as she realized her brother wasn't in the room. She told herself he was probably just in his room or the library, not wanting to see anyone, but something in her gut said something was wrong.

"Dad," she interrupted, getting to her feet. Everyone turned towards her. "Leo's not here."

The moment she saw concern in her father's face, she knew she was right to be worried.

"Taylor Ann, why don't you check his room. I'll look in the library. The rest of you, spread out across the house and grounds. He needs to know what's happened," Heir said.

****

The house was large, but there were a lot of people looking, so it wasn't long before everyone was back in Heir's office, trying to keep themselves looking pleasant and unconcerned until the cameras were out of sight. The moment the door closed, however, all of the anxiety came to the surface.

Shianne gripped Aris's hand hard as everyone reported the same thing. Leo was gone. No one was entirely sure if there were things missing from his room because he was such a private person, but Taylor Ann seemed convinced that he'd packed a bag and gone somewhere. The others all agreed that was likely given the circumstances, but Shianne saw something on her father's face that made her wonder if he suspected something else. What that was, she didn't know, but it wasn't Leo taking off because he was upset.

"What we must decide now is what to do next." Heir's voice carried over the murmurs of the others. "Do we involve the authorities, or search for Leo on our own?"

"If we call the cops, the press is going to find out," Erickson pointed out. "And that might make Leo try harder to hide."

"Or they could mob him," Pru spoke up. Her expression was abnormally somber. "Think about all the attention we've gotten since the fire. People know someone died. If we tell people that Leo's run away they're going to think he's guilty of something or they're going to realize he's the one who lost somebody."

"He's never had to handle the press up close," Taylor Ann said. "They'll eat him alive."

"So it's agreed," Heir said. "We look for Leo ourselves."

Everyone nodded.

"Where do we start?" Alexander asked the next obvious question. He'd been quiet since the fire, but Shianne had noticed it was a different kind of quiet than before, like whatever had been dark inside him was gone. He wasn't the same flirty, funny little brother he had been before, but it was still an improvement over how he had been at the beginning of their trip.

"I think the first thing we need to do is not to panic," Di said, her voice crisp and business-like. "It's quite possible that Leo just needed some time to himself and he'll come back on his own. I suggest we give him the night and if he's not home in the morning, we begin to search. Heir and I will put together a list of places Leo could be and we'll share them with you tomorrow."

"You're really going to just leave him out there for the night?" Pru asked.

"He lost the woman he loved, Pru." Heir's voice was gentle. "It is not something a person gets over easily. Sometimes, we need to get away."

Shianne swallowed hard and Aris's fingers tightened around her hand. She couldn't imagine what her brother was going through. If she'd lost Aris, she would've been devastated. For Leo, it was so much worse. Saraleti hadn't just been his first love, but she'd been the only person he'd truly loved since his mother had died. Shianne just hoped, wherever he was, her little brother was okay.

She tapped her grandmother on her shoulder as the others filed out of the room. "May I speak to you for a moment?" Rupa nodded and followed Shianne and Aris down the hall to the library. Once they were inside, she turned to face them, preparing herself for what she had to say.

"You want us to wait until Leo's found," Rupa said it for her.

Shianne nodded. "I know you were planning on going home at the beginning of next week, and if Leo's found by then, it'll be different, but I can't plan to leave while he's gone."

"I understand," her grandmother said. "And I have decided that we will stay to help with the search."

"Really?"

"Don't sound so surprised, Shianne." Rupa's tone was gently chiding. "He is my grandson."

"I-I..."

"Although I suppose I should not have spoken for Aris," Rupa said, saving Shianne the embarrassment of having to apologize. "It is no longer my place to do so." She looked at him. "Will you be staying?"

Aris nodded. "I will not leave until Leo is home safe."

"Then it's settled." Rupa opened the door. "Now, I suggest we all get some sleep. We may very well have long days ahead of us."

Shianne looked up at Aris as her grandmother left. She might have long, uncertain days ahead, but at least he'd be there with her. The thought would've been enough to make her smile if she hadn't been so worried about Leo.

CHAPTER TWENTY-EIGHT

When he'd seen the stories on the news and heard the first reports that someone had died, he'd thrown up, sure that Alexander was gone. He'd seen the tabloid pictures of the blond Vamp in Europe and had known that things were bad. He didn't know how bad, but the emptiness he'd seen in Alexander's eyes had broken his heart. He'd told himself then that it wasn't his problem anymore, but then came the fire. Noah had sat in front of the television, waiting to see a glimpse of Alexander, but the wall of police had been thick and the Scottish reporters hadn't been able to get close enough. Five excruciating hours before the official press release saying that the Vamp family was all safe and accounted for, that the young woman who had died had been a family friend, a ballerina from France.

He'd kept his phone with him for the next two days, waiting for a phone call he knew he was foolish to expect. Alexander had no reason to call him. The two of them had made it perfectly clear where they'd stood with each other that night in London. It still didn't stop Noah's heart from skipping a beat every time his phone rang, or the pain of disappointment when it wasn't *him*.

Then he'd seen on the news that the Vamps had returned to Beverly Hills. He'd paced in the hotel room where the company had put him up for his LA shoot, arguing with himself that he needed to stay away. The argument hadn't lasted very long.

****

When the knock came, Alexander knew it would be Pru. After the fire, Pru had told him that staying angry seemed so petty after what had happened to Saraleti, and he had promised her that he'd never push her away again. They'd held each other at the funeral, eerily similar to the way he'd held her when their mother's body had been taken away. He'd been her rock then and they'd been each other's now.

He opened the door, ready to invite her in for whatever talk she needed, but the words died in his mouth the second he registered who was standing on the other side.

He put his hand on the doorframe, suddenly needing something to steady him. "Noah?" The name was a whisper.

"I saw the fire on the news," he said. "And I had to make sure you were okay. Pru just told me about Leo. I'm so sorry."

Alexander knew he should say something. Thank Noah for being a friend. Tell him that everything was okay. But when he opened his mouth to speak, nothing came out. Instead, the reality of everything that had happened came crashing down at once.

The night he'd taken the models to bed and lost Noah.

Knowing he'd done the unforgivable by sleeping with Scott.

The emptiness he couldn't fill.

The agony of watching Noah walk onto the elevator with the model.

The self-loathing he'd tried to get rid of with men and pain.

How he'd worried his family.

The way he'd treated his beloved baby sister.

The fear when he'd seen the fire, not knowing who would survive.

Seeing Leo broken and not being able to fix it.

And now Noah was here and all Alexander wanted to do was kiss him and tell him how sorry he was, but he knew what he'd done could never be forgiven.

"Hey, shh, it's okay." Noah's arms were suddenly around him. "I'm here."

Alexander buried his face against Noah's neck, breathing deeply, wanting to have the scent ingrained in his mind. Noah's hand brushed over Alexander's hair and the vampire heard the door close. He raised his head and Noah's mouth was on his. He knew he should resist, that Noah just felt sorry for him, but he wasn't strong enough.

Then Noah was pulling back and he knew it was over. But Noah didn't move to the door. Instead, he took Alexander's hand and gently pulled him back to the bed. Wild hope leaped inside him and Alexander pushed it down. He might not be strong enough to resist, but he wouldn't make more of this than it was.

They undressed each other without a word, letting their hands remember each other's bodies. It was sweet and tender, and everything Alexander needed, but when they were done and Alexander was wrapped around Noah's body, he knew the time had come to speak.

Noah's eyes were closed, but Alexander knew the human wasn't asleep. He ran his fingers through Noah's hair and the younger man pressed himself back more firmly against Alexander's chest. Perhaps, he thought, it would be easier to do this without Noah looking at him.

"I need to tell you something."

Noah went still.

"First, I need to say I'm sorry, for everything. You were right that I was scared. I still am. I'm absolutely petrified about my feelings for you. I thought I could forget you, and I tried my damnedest to do just that. And all I ended up doing was hating myself. I did things, let people do things to me, that I'm ashamed of. I just wanted the pain to go away, and it never did." Alexander ran his hand over Noah's shoulder, trying to memorize the soft skin and firm muscles. "The night of the fire, when I saw what happened to Saraleti and I saw how devastated Leo was, I knew that the reason I couldn't fill the emptiness inside me was because it's you. You're the only one I want, the only one I ever want to be with."

Noah rolled onto his back so that he was looking up at Alexander.

"I don't know if this was pity sex, or 'glad to see you're not dead' sex, but I don't want it to be that." Alexander brushed his fingertips across Noah's cheek. "Is there any way we can forget everything and just start over?"

Noah's face was serious and when he shook his head, Alexander insides twisted painfully. "No, we can't ignore the past." He reached up and put his hand on Alexander's cheek, and this time, it was the vampire who went motionless. "But we can learn from it and move forward." His thumb brushed across Alexander's lips. "Make a future together?"

Alexander bent his head and took Noah's mouth in a kiss so intense that it left them both breathless. When they broke apart, Noah wrapped his arms around Alexander's waist and put his head on the vampire's shoulder. Alexander pulled the human tight against him, never wanting to let him go again.

"You know," he said quietly. "There was one other thing I did that I think you should know about." He felt Noah stiffen in his arms. "It was really stupid."

Noah tilted his head back.

Alexander smiled. "I fell for a human."

The smile that lit up Noah's face chased away the last of the darkness in Alexander's soul.

"That's good," Noah said. "Because I did something pretty stupid too. I fell for a vampire."

Alexander chuckled and the two burrowed under the sheets, closing themselves off from the world outside and all its problems. Those would come with the morning, but the night was theirs.

****

Pru was up early. Her concern for Leo would not let her sleep much. She changed out of her pajamas and stretched out on her bed with her laptop. She hadn't checked any social media since the fire, not wanting to have to relive that night, but now she was going online. She had to see if she could figure out where Leo might have gone.

The first thing she saw was the screaming headline, "LEO VAMP MISSING." She swore and read the article. The reporter's anonymous source was obviously one of the camera crew. Apparently, Leo wasn't as invisible as he had been before the trip and his absence had been noticed. Heir and Di were going to be pissed.

Then she saw the links to the videos.

Pru's jaw dropped as she saw hundreds of people lining the streets. The streets in front of their New York home. In front of the network offices. In front of this house. Hundreds upon hundreds of people holding signs that all asked the same question.

Where was Leo Vamp?